Adamczewski's stories are quiet and feral, her imagery thrilling, the voices troubling and funny. There is calmness here but there is also wild power- a writer to pay attention to.

EVIE WYLD

This is an incredible collection of short stories: smart, surprising, fresh, strange and utterly unlike anything you've read before.

RACHEL LONG

Vida Adamczewski is one to watch, her style is fresh, authentic and provocative, her storytelling is vivid, concise and compelling, *Amphibian And Other Bodies* blew me away, I loved it and highly recommend you read Vida now.

SALENA GODDEN

Amphibian and Other Bodies is a rare treasure. Dazzlingly inventive, alarming, and funny. Stories slip and slide between the human and the more-than-human; the real and the fantastical. Frogs nest in the damp curls of sun-drenched girls; slugs slime their eggs into the ears of sleeping dogs; giant seahorses tear themselves from human wombs. Adamczewski's sentences shine and squelch: beautiful and alive.

CHARLIE GILMOUR

Amphibian and Other Bodies extends through time and space violently. From the strangeness of the cellular, to the use of overpriced Ubers, to the endeavour of feminine endurance. Adamczewski writes a stark declaration of the body as harmonious yet discordant territory.

EVE ESFANDIARI-DENNEY

Vida Adamczewski has retained in her writing the molten perceptions and synaesthetic imagination of childhood, and with them she has crafted a collection of tales that are by turns strange, charming, uneasy, acidic - and always unique.

ROB DOYLE

AMPHIBIAN
& OTHER BODIES

Amphibian and Other Bodies
Vida Adamczewski
TG0019

Second edition | Published 2024
100% Recycled & unbleached paper
Printed in the UK

Edited by Ned Green
Design by William Francis Green
Photography by Jack Davison

First edition launched in London | 23rd November 2023

toothgrinder.co.uk
toothgrinderuk@gmail.com
@toothgrinderpress

PREFACE

This book is not an inventory of your body. It does not keep a record of your moles. It does not know when your last bowel movement was, nor what it meant. Do not spit on it. It cannot tell what vitamins you need or how Jewish your grandfather was. Its dimensions are 129mm x 198mm. If you eat less, it will not shrink. Hold it in one hand, and test it in the air. This is the weight of it. The only way to make it lighter is to rip the pages out. Put your first finger on the tip of your nose. See. Your body is not in this book. Do not look for it here.

Frog walked into the house. It was dark. All the shutters were closed.

    'Toad, where are you?' called Frog.

    'Go away,' said the voice from a corner of the room.

Arnold Lobel, *Frog and Toad Are Friends*

AMPHIBIAN

Amphibian (adj) living both in water and on land. From the
Ancient Greek ἀμφίβιος (amphíbios), meaning "both kinds of life"

CAST

Woman (f)
Body (f)
Lecturer (m)

Director's Note -

AMPHIBIAN takes place in five locations; a lecture theatre; a woman's flat; a hospital examination table; within the body; in a pond. These environments have a peculiar tendency to seep into each other. If you are feeling nauseous or unable to tell the difference between what is real and what is not real, seek out the rhythm of the language. It is your anchor.

I.

BODY

Once I was a cluster of lilac frogspawn in the wet middle of
my mother. And all the eggs I have nestled inside me, going
off, were with me inside her too. In the deep pink of the belly,
I uncurled myself until my head bobbed on a narrow bony
stalk and my fingers fanned out from fin-like stumps and
my lungs grew fleshy and I kicked my feet to the edges and I
wriggled til the little mesh of capillaries made me blush and
all over I was covered, for a time, in fine fur and caul.

Then I was peering over the shoulder of the world, milk sick
dribbling down my chin. I was a scrunched tissue shoved
to my face and paper stitches on my forehead. I was ice
packs and blue paper hand towels wetted and slapped onto
purple knees. I was the sandpapery cough every Autumn
that had me barking like a seal and sloshed me with white
bile and dizzy spells. I was all the little phlegmy illnesses of
childhood. I was snotting into my dad's heroic hand when he
couldn't conjure a Kleenex.

I was nosebleeds, hundreds of them, soaking through pillow
cases and bath towels, bedsheets with big yellow roses soon
spattered with purplish brown. I was endless head back pinch
the bridge of my nose, making mud from the dust scuffed
up by sports day. Endless, can I be excused. I was endless red
skid marks in books and waiting for my father to collect me
from reception. Sit and roll my ankles outside the office, tilt
back on a squeaky chair, hunch over, hair veiled round my
face, and the blood gushing out of my nostrils, cracked and

raw, hot red stuff pooling in my cupped hands and trickling down, through the diamond gaps between my fingers, sticky on my lizard cold skin until the last gobs clot, and swing lethargically in thin strings, inches above the ground, and the tar of it darkens on the toes of my shoes.

I was flat as a paving stone, fifteen pipetting dye onto slivers of onion and my eye pressed painfully against a microscope, under the white light of the science lab, and searching the hazy trance of pink for elegance, for design. I was sucking the wet out of cucumber chunks and thinking too loudly about sex.

I was sixteen suddenly, still with clean white knickers and forgetting to wear a vest on PE changing days. Chasing my breath in the dank fug of grown up sweat and petally aerosols that left lines of white powder on sports braed chests. I was wishing to be older and waiting for the 7:29 train to Victoria in a shrunken one pound jumper and a too short skirt, and the men who reeked of skunk asking how old I was, how much I'd cost.

I was tripping over myself to get in with the girls with braces who gave their Catholic boyfriends head. I was drawing rough diagrams of ventricles and labelling aortas and pacing at the back of the room, the smell of formaldehyde surging up my nose, down my throat, scalpel clattering and my chin ricocheting off the edge of the desk. Top lip burst, and metal on my tongue. I was afraid of blood, unless it splashed out of my nose. All the other stuff made me woozy as a ghoul. I was relieved each month it did not come.

I was the horror of blood one day. The pain that gripped me by my sides. I was the stab every month of my budding ovary. The monthly bloating fear of appendicitis. Slumped on the toilet. A drop of blood blooming in the water, like a jellyfish, knee tremoring, head lolling forwards and the gooseflesh rising over my stomach, tugging at my shoulder blades. My whole body intended to the ground, draining out.

I was invited to the party. I was a meaty finger pressing up through my tights in the cider swill of a garden, the onion smell on my neck and the yanking of my plait. I was a boy, and another boy, and a boy sat with his hands folded in his lap like wilting flowers.

I was him, soft and sloppy, with his sweat slicked curls dangling above me. My eyes meeting the wall, and my lying, supine and stilled with spatchcocked hips. I was empty except for him, straining inside me. I was certain that inside was not so close, really.

How slippery that trick of saying no. If he would just cease, and scatter himself like dandelion flock. The insistence of his heart beating and the wet crunch of my bones, rocking, back and forth. With a sticky palm, his lifting my cheek and trying to meet my eye. He retrieves himself from me and I, the quiet, the lying there for a while.

The breaching of my glassy edge begins. I would hide in the loo if there was not a queue. I lick up rude tears. I stand on the stairs instead, hovering in an active pose, so everyone who sees me might believe I am with urgent purpose, merely passing through.

I am going to be sick. A violent limpid spew. The medicinal
burr of vodka catches in my nose. A stomach spasm crumples
me, spine like a drawstring, and my lips bloom blue. Ears
pop like I'm a plane, in a tunnel, muffled sound of party,
one, two, rush of cars, siren wail, rhythmic thumping
through the walls, exam hall hush, clock ticking, trains,
the ambient drone of a DJing never boyfriend in a dark
club, one day soon, chewing, spitting, stretching out, joints
clicking, scribbling of prescriptions for the pill, gossip, films,
underwater warble, gush of jumping in a pond and -

BODY
I am twenty-two.

WOMAN
Plopped here.

BODY
And now I am in situ -

LECTURER
we can begin.

II.

LECTURER
The African Clawed Frog, or Xenopus Laevis, is one of the most widely used model organisms in biological research. This is in large part because of the frog's close evolutionary relationship with humans.

WOMAN
Your eyes are kind of far apart. It's nice.

BODY
Blinking himself back into the world, the acrid smell of him, rising, the licked twists of hair in his armpit.

WOMAN
He knows I've been awake, watching.

BODY
The furore of your breathing, the lub dub lub dub of your heart, your eyelash fritzing in your dream.

WOMAN
I curl back into him, fibbing that I'm snoozing still

LECTURER
Male Xenopus have a mating call of long and short trills. Females also respond vocally, either signalling their acceptance with a rapping sound, or their rejection – more of a slow ticking – of the male

BODY

All the hubbub of the world diminished to the babble of his gut, as it eddies in the oyster of my ear.

WOMAN

I will miss this bit of hair, the island of it, here, on his hip

LECTURER

Of the seven amplexus modes – the positions in which frogs mate – African Clawed Frogs breed in inguinal amplexus; the male clasps the female in front of the female's back legs and squeezes until eggs come out.

BODY

when I guide him into me, will him into soft sounds, and when I kiss him on his clammy brow

WOMAN

I try to hold in my mind how I love him and kiss that into him like a seal pushing into warm wax.

BODY

Catch of my dry skin on his chin

WOMAN

Though it is him that will be on a plane tomorrow, it is me that is leaving

BODY

He puts his finger in his mouth and finds me again

WOMAN
Again

BODY
now kind of staggering through the thicket of my brain, can't place it, yet, the pulsing epicentre of this – tick tick

WOMAN
I hold his head on my breast for a second and feel the sea fret of his breath. It is over, now, and silence, then, is best.

LECTURER
Xenopus has been used extensively in research for developmental biology. From observation of Xenopus embryos, we have gleaned vital insights into the epigenetics of cell fate specification, the development of vasculature and gut morphogenesis in human offspring. In fact, frogs were even taken into space in 1992 to test whether reproduction and embryonic development could occur normally in zero gravity.

BODY
Tick, Tick - I imagine it, the size of a newt, turning somersaults in the swamp of my womb. Latched on, sucking blood through its body, which is a straw, which is a balloon.

LECTURER
In 1930, in South Africa, Lancelot Hogben injects hormones from an Ox's pituitary gland into a female Xenopus. Soon after, the frog, without any contact with a male specimen, begins to lay eggs. Females have not been observed in the wild producing eggs spontaneously. Hogben immediately recognised the frog's sensitivity, its experimental tractability, and from here he really developed the Xenopus into the model organism we still use today.

WOMAN
Tick, tick, tick. Knickers yanked up. I pace the bathroom like an abandoned puppy. He is on the other side of a border now, in a lab, by a pond, making notes on how things grow. Tick, I keep checking, as the damp creeps across the test strip, tick. Minutes yet. I set a timer on my phone and pull the cord to switch the bathroom light off, on, off. The fan comes on with a hush.

LECTURER
But though I have a soft spot for Hogben – he once famously declared that he disliked "football, economists, eugenicists, Fascists, Stalinists and Scottish conservatives" – research and seminal discoveries have been miscredited to him. Hogben did not make the leap.

It was his student, South African scientist, Hillel Shapiro who deduced that, given that urine of pregnant people contains hormones from the pituitary gland, and the Xenopus had this extraordinary reaction to hormones from Oxen, that the Xenopus, African Clawed Frogs, could be used to identify – even very early – pregnancy.

BODY
In the deepest shiver of this evening, in its glassiest stare, in the reflection of the mirror in the window, I have seen you, you are growing there, from under my jaw like an ingrown hair, like a swollen gland, a tumour, and I cannot bear the thrumming of your heart, it seems to toll from everywhere. Tick, tick, tick

LECTURER

*Identifying pregnancy, up until this point, had been a loose
hanging together of science and superstition. HCG, a hormone
only found in pregnant people, had been identified in 1920. And
tests had been developed involving mice. (The mice were injected
with urine and days later dissected to measure the growth of their
ovaries.) Similar tests used rabbits and rats. But these tests were
time consuming, pernickety, and imprecise. And they required the
death of the test animal.*

*Periods and symptoms had been tracked of course by people with
uteruses, for millennia, but there are many reasons that the
monthly -- menses -- might cease.*

WOMAN

Tick, tick, It's midnight, I think, the room is swamped in
blue light as I scroll through the apocalypse, get advertised
some articles I might also like, and asked by the Guardian,
once again, to donate. A clear blue advert pops up. A woman,
dubbed in english, giggles the gorgeous news to her best,
shiny haired, friend. Oh baby, baby

LECTURER

*The "Hogben test", or the Shapiro test rightly called, by
comparison, proved simple and reliable. Inject a sample of
human urine under the skin of a female frog and if the person is
pregnant, within hours, the frog will produce a handful of white,
globular spawn.*

*African Clawed Frogs were plentiful, they were easily and
cheaply farmed. Isolated colonies of them were established all over
the world, for use in research and testing. Thousands were injected*

with urine. Babies were born. The frogs were not harmed by the
process and could be used again and again. The first mainstream
pregnancy test had been invented, and it

BODY
is strange.

LECTURER
Of course, handling live frogs is less than practical. So, after
decades of research, the frog has been distilled

WOMAN
into a plastic stick for me to piss on. And here we are,
waiting. Tick, tick, tick.

LECTURER
Yes, I'll take questions

WOMAN
What happens next?

BODY
Don't you know

WOMAN
The minutes have elapsed and the furred pink lines
present themselves.
Pregnant. Tick.

BODY
In a pond somewhere, a frog blinks.

III.

WOMAN

He calls me in the evenings. I put him on speaker, while
I open and close windows, get into and out of a bath, his
voice echoes round the flat, stirring the papery leaves of the
spider plant, parched to white in his absence. I let him speak,
uninterrupted. He asks me what I think about the virus, the
locusts in Africa, the droughts and the fires and the floods of
acid rain. I am terrible on the phone, croaking like a toad. He
says Men bloody ruin everything. He says we are worse than
God. The virus will mutate. I say I don't know.

Though he's out of sight, he is still too close. He keeps
cropping up, like a head louse scratch, like a ghost. It is in his
absence that I have felt him most about the place, this house,
since he has left it and left his socks crisping behind the
radiator and his unsightly books of diagrams and brain scans,
curled with licked corners and underlinings, scraps of paper
trapped between pages, just waiting, saving his place.

BODY

He is long gone, crouching over quadrants of mud, picking
around in the slime of stagnant ponds. Things stretched out
on trays.

WOMAN

But he was earnest and green jumpered for the most part. I
liked him a lot.

A particular morning I remember. His arm had stiffened
beneath me. I rolled to the cold edge of the bed, and, leaving

him my body as a courtesy, I took a turn around the room. I
live away from my body sometimes. It is easier not to be in it.

He reaches for me and bleary eyed he speaks

LECTURER
Where have you gone?

BODY
I am all looking, noting the spittle crust round his bottom lip
and his goodness, my mouth moves air noiselessly from my
inside to my outside like the gill of a fish. Still, he is beyond
the glass of me.

WOMAN
With the conciliatory desperation of a father presented with
a barely grazed knee,

LECTURER
We'll go for a walk will we? Have some breakfast?

WOMAN
He has eggs, in a cardboard crown on the kitchen counter.

LECTURER *and* **BODY**
*They say your body is a brain. You don't have to think to move
your arm, you just move it. I suppose, he reaches his arm out in
front of him, clenches his fist, splays his fingers, turns his palm
into the sun, I empathise. It's like when you wake up and you've
got a dead arm. It is weird, when you think about it. To be
embodied. I say*

WOMAN

Yes, it is.

He mashed an egg in a cup with a fork, butter and salt, and spooned it onto toast for me.

BODY

Barely chewed, just swallowed and inside me now and soon, silently, without my noticing, without any naming at all, merely the unceremonious transubstantiation of digestion, its protein becomes mine.

LECTURER

The Xenopus is tongueless and toothless. They use their hands to push food into their mouths and down their throats. They are scavengers and will eat almost anything they can fit into their gobs. They eat their own larvae, frequently, which has allowed them to survive in areas with limited food supply.

BODY

The cells split and doubled, cloned themselves. Amino acids were transported, formed new chains. He knew about these things of mine, the neurons like roots, the ribbons of bodies, the webs and sinews that hold my guts in place, about oxygen and salts being passed across membranes. In a rapid stream, he speaks of all these things and then how

LECTURER

Human beings are the only animals who can be so absent from any moment, so caught up in their heads, so wracked with anxiety that they don't know, instinctively, anything true or nice about the world.

BODY

And just then he says

LECTURER

I had a moment there this morning, next to you in bed. Totally content, totally present, and everything sounded beautiful even that siren, that car horn outside breaking the air

WOMAN

he said it was like his brain was a slice of bread

BODY

soaking in milk.

LECTURER

African Clawed Frogs are not terribly active. When they are not feeding, or mating, they sit motionless on the bed of the pond, or float at the top with their heads sticking out.

WOMAN

He was too soft. He was as soft as moss. As gossamer, as blossom shaken from a tree, and swept by the breeze into gutter drifts. He was as soft as peach rot. So, I sent him off

BODY

away

WOMAN

and good.

BODY

Better.

WOMAN

His work. That's the reason

BODY

Mostly, He was nice to have about.

WOMAN

I don't know how to cope with being seen by a face like that.

BODY

His eyes were round. His brittle mouth.

WOMAN

That focused gaze that lingers on me, naked.

BODY

The first thing I noticed about being loved is that you are
totally exposed.

WOMAN

His gaze doesn't strip me to the skin, not naked, like come
hither bedroom eyes, but more like he has taken a razor and
he's shaved all the hair off my head and he's taking a scalpel
and winching my scalp open, taking little samples of my
grey matter to analyse at a later date, naked. Naked like a
thousand abrasive questions -

BODY

But it's not that –

WOMAN

It's just that when someone looks at you, and really looks
at you, unrelentingly, they're sending these beams of light
direct from their eyes straight into the very red centre of you
and you have to find some way to deflect them or diffract
them otherwise you're just gonna go fucking blind. And I
want to break eye contact, more than anything, to shatter
that meditation on my soul, with a scream, to pierce that
migrainous quiet. The relentless imparting of care to feed
this thing, which might be love, or might not be anything so
specific. My raging and my blundering as you try to hold me
and I lash out, arms outstretched to keep you back,

BODY

a distance,

WOMAN

and I, in abject terror, squirming, horror at my flesh, my
mind, the men, this unspooling that begins from the jelly of
the egg. And as my jaw locks and my tongue retreats into my
throat and my tear ducts swell, and I prepare to disintegrate,
to smash, break like a wave against him who probes the most
tender parts of me I found instead, he said my name enough
to remind me of who I am, I am

BODY

"mostly water"

WOMAN

I am now the need of him. I am the want

BODY
the shivering, hiccup, heave

WOMAN
Breathe. Breathe.

BODY
the heart that beats

WOMAN
in waiting

BODY
beats

WOMAN
I stop answering the phone.

BODY
Better with him gone.

WOMAN
Better to be alone.

IV.

BODY

To grow, to grow, to grow, to grow, to grow, to grow, to grow, to grow, to grow, to grow, to grow...

I am bone knackered, marrow swolled, aching, itching, yawning in my breast the smell of day to day stings my nose intense as hay, as butcher shop, as bruising fruit. Pungent funk of him lingers still stale on the sheet. I sweat, turn circles in the night, push my fist into my diaphragm, with each breath, resist. In the ooze of me, a flutter of blood cells worm through, through, to there, where a tiny speck pushed in, dug roots, and sugaring, chewing, thickened to maroon, as night seeps in like fog...

LECTURER

a decade or so after the African Clawed Frog is first injected with urine – around the same time the pill is being unethically trialled – around the same time that abortion is being reluctantly decriminalised – in the thorny corridors of universities, anthropologists and evolutionary biologists begin exchanging explanations for the high morbidity of pregnancy and childbirth.

BODY

and in my fitful sleep, the blood slipping along its tributaries to the deep of me, where new strangeness is growing, growing, drawing my attention like the red pulse round a wound

LECTURER

The explanation that is settled on – a theory you might be familiar with – is that when human beings began to walk on two legs, our pelvises shrank. And, simultaneously our brains had evolved to be so complex, and so large

BODY

ungainly

LECTURER

That our skulls could not be safely birthed. The body's solution is to give birth earlier, to less mature embryos, before their brains have grown too big for the birth canal. It's reasoned that this is why human babies emerge dependent on their caregivers

BODY

spongey skulled.

LECTURER

In 1960, an anthropologist called Sherwood Washburn christens this theory: The Obstetric Dilemma. It becomes a kind of folklore, being such a seductive theory that we were foiled by our own evolutionary advances, by our biological hubris.

BODY

I'd like to make it clear, I had no intention

LECTURER

But more recent research indicates that the anthropologists got it wrong. Firstly, the human pelvis varies widely in size, and its width doesn't seem to affect how well we walk.

Secondly, Humans do not give birth prematurely. In fact, compared with apes of similar size, human pregnancies last about 37 days longer than we would expect.

BODY
To grow, to grow, to grow, incessantly

LECTURER
The fact is that growing a body, and particularly growing a human brain, requires a lot of energy. As the foetus's brain grows larger, it demands more and more fuel, more and more sustenance from the mother, its host. The last few weeks of pregnancy, it is almost impossible for the mother to eat enough to keep the foetus nourished. The mother's body is pushed to the upper limit of possible sustainable metabolic rates in humans. In other words,

BODY
It has to end at some point.

V.

WOMAN

I have never kept track of my periods, no red dots or crosses
in my diary, so when the woman from the abortion service
asks me over the phone when my last period started, I just
said: I don't know. There was a pause, a crackle on the line,
politer than a sigh, but strained nonetheless.

Given the ambiguity, I am summoned to the hospital
for tests. I wait in the blue zone, my dingy cotton mask
stretched over my nose, holding a warm plastic jar of my own
piss. The blue zone is a holding room with rows and rows of
grey chairs, arranged like pews.

BODY

There were blue lines painted on the linoleum floor and fish
shaped stickers on the wall that directed my feet here. There
are only a few of us in the room, waiting. We shift in our
seats in similar rhythms, heft our legs over our knees, swing
our feet, tap our toes.

WOMAN

The nurse at the desk beckons me over. I push my piece of
paper, now seamed with folding and refolding, across the
desk. There is a clipboard and another form to fill out.

Receptionist
A doctor will be with you soon.

BODY

I lower myself onto a chair, and begin to wait again. My mask itches on my left cheek. I can smell the fur of my unbrushed teeth.

WOMAN

The doctor and I wait while a stick she has stirred in my urine like tea changes colour. I think of the African Clawed Frog, excreting its eggs with a placid grin.

Doctor

So, you are pregnant.

I nod. The doctor indicates the grey bed, and invites me to lie down, asks me to lift up my dress and roll my tights down to my hips.

Doctor

Do you want to see?

WOMAN

not particularly.

BODY

The gel is cold and I am tender, aware of my bladder, as the scanner presses and rolls over me.

Doctor

It must be a very early pregnancy

WOMAN

There is nothing to see. The doctor asks me to take my tights and knickers off. She summons a nurse from the corridor to assist. The doctor brandishes a long white probe now, and her other hand is held in that strange swan neck pose doctors assume to stop themselves nonchalantly touching their sleeves and contaminating wounds. She uses her elbow awkwardly to lift the white sheet that is perched on my knees.

BODY

There is a pushing against my hymen,

Doctor

this might be uncomfortable

WOMAN

I withhold the wince. It's fine. Fine.

BODY

My chest stilled, bubble in my throat. I clench my teeth.

WOMAN

Breathe.

BODY

Inside, within, the quickening.

WOMAN

The doctor reels off some statistics that the nurse punches in.

BODY

Egg sac yolk not visible a lathering stream of numbers,
impossibly small all zero point three recurring like
calculators in exams at school. I am the searing and the
pinch, as she pushes in another inch. This right ovary is
larger by a millimetre - I could have said. It stings. I send
my brain away, elsewhere, as I have learnt to do. To hear me
being measured, and inputted into a beige computer with
clattering keys, to be become a patient, 'the mother', who
does not exist beyond what has been tabulated and counted
up, measured before, again, in rooms exactly like this. I send
my brain away and for a while

WOMAN

everything is silence and white light.

BODY

For these past weeks of gravidity, I have been as old and
dowdy as a gristled sow. I am head spun each time I stand,
left breast all throb and pang.

WOMAN

The quiet distrust of this body settles in my stomach like
blood. We are quite different. Quite against my wishes, my
womb is always seeking sperm so it can replicate itself within
itself and I am a bewildered spectator, a parasite myself
embedded in the walls of this body, all limbs, and strange
machinations. I cannot stand to think of the watery tapioca
in my uterus covertly forming tissue, bones and things that
might one day grow into a girl looking up at the cracks that
spider across the ceiling from the big light. Blink away.

BODY

Watch the yellow circles dance in your eyes.

WOMAN

Back in the body, back in the room.

BODY

The light winks twice, I am pinned down, she grinds her
teeth and seizes against my squirming, pulsing like a medusa
in the nape of my neck, my abdominals throb and slide, and
the Doctor sliding away deeper into me scouting this way,
that, the pressure of this instrument, the hard outside, feeling
its way through the tender flesh along my bowel, the bruise
and rising bile I wish I could say get it out of me

WOMAN

get it out right now

Doctor

All done, you can pop your clothes back on.

WOMAN

A plastic shower curtain is drawn across the room to
protect my modesty, my bare buttocked fanny out indignity.
Considerate. Though, given that I've had my legs splayed in
stirrups, arse shunted right to the edge of the bed, hanging
off, and her probe plunged inside me, scouting about, the
niceties now seem absurd.

BODY

Hammering heart, my fingers are clumsy and trembling, as
they feel their way back to me

WOMAN

get a grip, how long does it take to put bloody tights on.

BODY

Jamming my many toed feet into a nylon knot, that clings on and drags around my sweaty legs. I slip

WOMAN

out from behind the curtain, and I stand beside the doctor, apologetically, as we wait for the printer. All the while, slime seeping out into the pouch of my knickers squishy squashy crawling up the crack of my arse, down my thigh, like semen when I stand up for a wee in the night.

Doctor

six weeks, or thereabouts

WOMAN

The doctor seals my referral letter in an envelope to return to the abortion service. She will email too.

The lift descends and clinks to a stop. A man with a slip of paper which I read between his fingers says he has permission to visit his daughter. A new born. He looks shocked to see me standing in the lift and clutches wildly at his pockets for a mask. Finding nothing, he holds the letter over his mouth and steps in. I say don't worry. He still says sorry. Twice.

BODY

I wonder at the droplets suspended in the air now that we have exchanged words and for a brief moment I feel

high, elated, my skin glistening. I am indeed a spectator,
I am flotsam and jetsam in these corridors, carried by the
current of bureaucracy and fuss that manages my body, me,
the parts of me that are filed away, typed up, living in petri
dishes, the photos, and numbers, the detailed documents and
transcribed testimonies, the paper trail that is the ultimately
the rub of who I am, siphoned off, delivered to people who
are more expert on my specifics than me. Peace.

WOMAN

Peace because there is a cogent beauty here; a man desperate
to see his baby breathing in her glass bowl and I, a vessel for
another gloop that twitches on the monitor, which I should
not have seen, should not have been angled towards me, and
the absurdity of being titled mother: age: 22: when I am
none of these things.

BODY

Just a body made of cells that are not 22 at all, none of
whom were with me when I was born, except, I suppose, the
ones that might grow into their own bodies, like this one
now, this frogspawn thing

WOMAN

that I am going to indelicately ejaculate next week, all
being well.

BODY

I am trapped briefly in a revolving door, before I slip into the
pedestrian swell.

VI.

WOMAN

Thursday. Back to the clinic. So much for pills by post.
Every extra hurdle, extra moment playing host to the
zygote, my insides feel further from me. They are concerned
about my anaemia –

BODY

my fainting spells, my occasional bloody nose.

WOMAN

The night before the appointment, I do not sleep. Tiredness
gnaws at my brow but does not breach me. I lie in bed and
once again staring at the ceiling, I think about being sixteen.
I think about that boy's thing inside me. I think about
my biology lessons, and wandering through the science
museum's exhibition on 'love'. How spider plants make
clones of themselves, how snails drug each other, and the
balletic mucus twirl of slugs, of foxes screeching in the park.

And after dark, the unlit paths you walk down, with one
eye scanning for rustling leaves, for footfalls of increasing
speed. I think about those boys I'd leave in the morning, the
years stacked up with brutes aggressively pursued and how
squirmingly vulnerable they looked, how sleepy they were
after, how depleted, how sapped.

I put my hand between my legs. I bring myself to the edge,
and yielding, the yawning feeling that precedes tears spreads
within me like a smog and I withdraw my hand to hold
myself around the waist.

And I am possessed by a single driving thought:

WOMAN *and* **BODY**
Get out. Get out.

BODY
It wriggles inside me.

LECTURER
The foetus has a sleep cycle.

WOMAN
When I close my eyes I see a fish-like alien, floating, silently,
and then its grey pearl eyes roll open. I cradle my stomach,
and try to imagine that it's a baby. With little hands and
feet, and soft skin, and downy hair, and a head that smells of
yeast, but all I see is a beast like an axolotl -

BODY
Get out

WOMAN
- bobbing asininely on its back, its see-through flesh, and
the feathery fronds that crown its head.

BODY
Out

LECTURER
The foetus is amphibian, soft boned and submerged in water.

WOMAN
I do not want to share a skin with it tonight.

VII.

BODY

When the nurse extends my arm, starts swabbing the tender hinge of my elbow and stretching the skin in search of

nurse

One second – your veins are tiny.

WOMAN

I am shuddering on the bed, teeth chattering and jiggling my leg, little whelps issue from my mouth like a puppy dreaming of being chased. Turn green. A garnet blob is dabbed away with a wad of cotton. The tears steal down my cheeks. The nurse tells me

nurse

don't be scared, it's all routine.

WOMAN

I grope for what she means –

BODY

meanwhile each capillary retreats from the surface of my skin.

nurse

a slight pinch

BODY

The pills come in a brown paper bag that crackles in my hand.

WOMAN

The first pill I take on the walk home, I lurch it into my throat before the beast reaches up and chokes away my will.

The next day, walking lengths of my local park, I feel it give.

BODY

Drop.

WOMAN

I feel nauseous, and a brief kind of ringing spasm of pain deep in my cervix. Then this flowering wetness, warm and heavy, in my knickers, soaking my trousers, running down my leg.

BODY

And the smell.

WOMAN

It didn't smell like period blood or piss. I can't summon that scent to my brain now, uncanny how the certainty prickled my neck. A dog that had nuzzled me inquisitively on a previous lap, backed away from me whimpering. That sound stuck, I can hear it now, and the fear that rippled through me, the dinky shame that wheedled up, of seeing that dog's primal distress of what mess was cradled in my gusset.

I lie in bed, pressing my fist into my abdomen to stop my cervix's yapping. Twisting myself into a spiral, knees hooked under my chin. Thick clots as mark the end of a nosebleed. I take two codeine, with water, and let them dissipate.

BODY

Breathe. Breathe. The pain relents.

WOMAN

I was alone in my body, then.

(*Silence. Hold it.*)

VIII.

WOMAN

A week later, the blood still eeking out. I head to the park,
phone in hand and thumb an email. On an out breath, I
press send. It whistles over the ether in flickering pixels,
pixie dust, undulating shimmer of mist drummed up by the
beating heat of sun.

I thought you might like to know.

I was away for a while, but I am come back, prodigal, and it
is like no time has passed at all, though I am very old, all of a
sudden, old as the hills, as a fossil, as a gorge, a fall, by turns I
even resemble my mother.

I am back now, and I am newly merged with the shivering
lace of nerves, the thick slabs of muscle that clutch my womb
in throw, I am the blood that ebbs and flows. The soft fat that
folds around my thighs and velvet brush of skin cells dead
and dried, I am the eggs that each month bud and traverse
my uterus, the piece of copper the nurse deftly thrust inside
me.

I am swimming in a pond beside my mother and the quick
divulging of my abortion to her patient heart, her holding
me and wishing she'd been there, to squeeze my hand, to
stroke the wisps of hair that glitter in the sun now, bright
with beads of water, I am floating in her eyes gazing back
at me, I am years on, years added, I am running for the bus,
running fingers over skin, coughing into elbows, breathing,
kissing, bleeding, hot flushed years, eating, dreaming years,

years embedded into me like sweat in gym-kit, I am here,
now, sitting on the bank, I am slipping under the water,
breathing, under water,

each breath fills me like a palm under a tap, scooped up and
swallowed down, the relief to breathe, to breathe behind my
belly button, the water chuckling round my ears, To slink
out, shake off, squelch of pond slime, green weeds, and mud
beneath my feet.

I reach up to shield my face from the sun. Star my hand and
see the light bleed through primordial, webbed swags of
skin. Turn it this way, that. I remember, with a grin. Like a
primate, a paw, a frog's foot with its sticky orbs, a fin. I can
make my hand - mutate - into a jellyfish, a bird, a spider
crawling on my leg, a fist. The size of a human heart, beating
out its rhythm on my breast.

BODY
OneTwo OneTwo OneTwo OneTwo

WOMAN
I lie back and breathe, bask in the indiscreetness of my body,
how it melts into the grass. I think I might settle here, in the
meadow of my own arms, with the dew scenting my skin, my
fingers wrinkling, and my eyes blinking with every breath.

BODY
Elsewhere, he crouches to inspect the mud. A frog scuttles
under a leaf. The bubble of its chest heaves. The foam of its
offspring in the water, rippled, lapping the edge, breathe —

(their voices joining together)

Breathe.
Breathe.

END

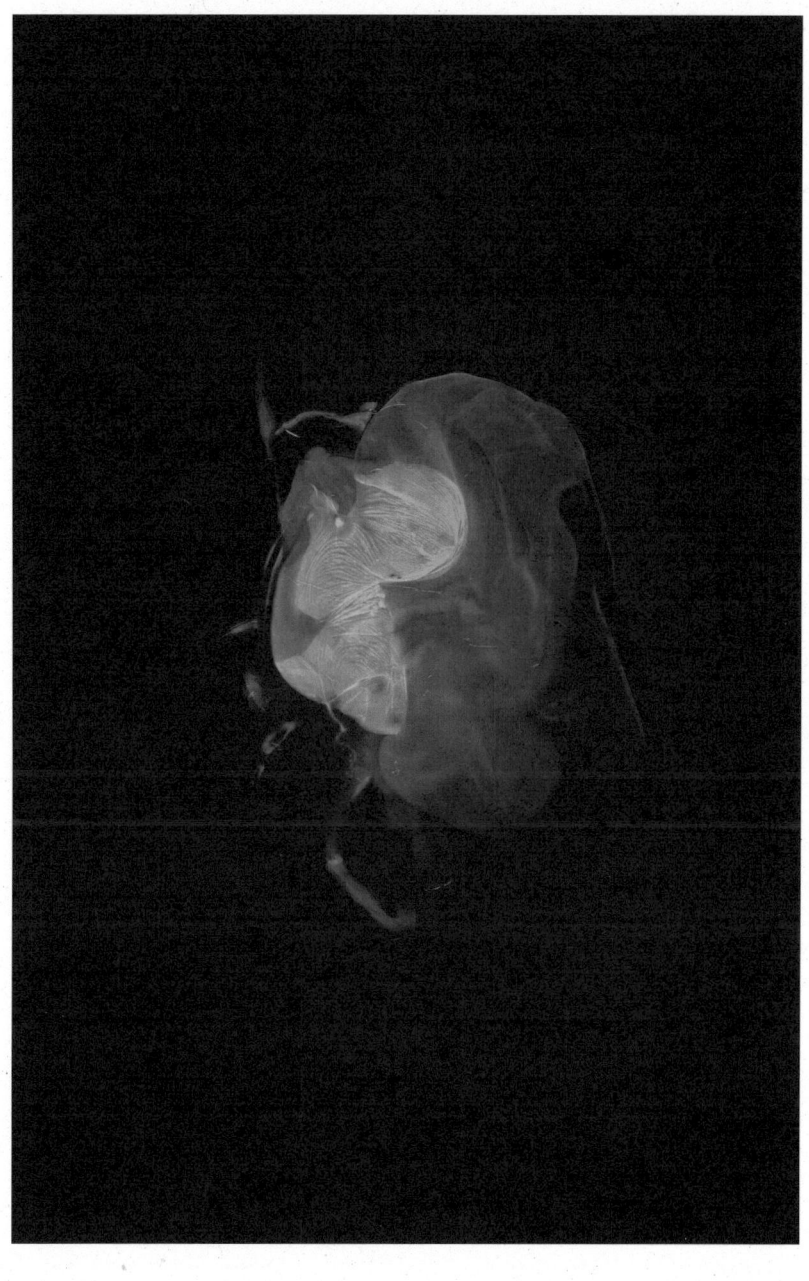

Dog

Yes, the dog was bad. Badly behaved, badly trained. The dog's breath was bad. The dog was bad at coming back, bad at lying down, bad at leaving be. The dog was bad mannered. She begged for food. She stole things and hid them. She was bad to some people too. She took badly against them and once she got it in her head she would not let it go. Instead she growled when they came near or jumped so that she knocked them back a step. She was a bad dog in all respects but one - and that was that the dog knew.

The dog was a street dog. The dog was found in an alley, moth-eaten by mange and licked silver with slug trails. Slugs slept inside the ears of the dog and laid their eggs there. The dog's ears were unhearing. At first, they heard all. They heard the rubber soled tread of approaching kitchen porters, swinging rubbish bags into the alley way. They heard the clatter of tins inside the bags and glass improperly wrapped shattering inside. They heard the hiskkk of one shard slicing the bag open, then the sag and slop of its innards spilling and dripping onto the tarmac. The dog commando crawled towards the mess, shuffling her nose in and letting her tongue lick lick. The dog's ears pricked to the swearing of the impatient chef, the door crashing open and the sudden silence as the figure sighs and lights a cigarette. The click, whoosh, ahhh. The dog's eyes flicked left and right. She drew her brows together and the long whiskery hairs on them scanned the air for dangers. Nothing large enough to tell the hairs it is coming. Scarier for the dog is Nothing.

The dog brings her ears down and back, close to the skull. The dog stays like this for many days. She sleeps, and as she sleeps her head lolls to the side. Her body slumps so it is flat against the tarmac. Ear against the ground, she hears the muffled rumble of traffic coming through the earth. Sleep comes over the dog. Sleep comes as many mice. They leave their fleas. After the mice, the slugs come. Inching over the dog, barely ruffling her hair. In the morning, the dog wakes to an alien oozing, then a sound like bubbles bursting, pop pop pop. Then silence. The eardrum of the dog is lacquered over with slug glue. The dog is afraid to move. In the new snow-quiet of the world, the dog just twitches her eyebrows. The slugs make themselves at home, shitting out their eggs into the hollows between the stalactites of the dog's finely tuned ear. The dog tucks her head beneath a paw and closes her eyes. When the bin men come, all clatter and smash, and friendly shouts, resonant with purpose, the dog hears nothing. When the bags are lifted away, and swung into the truck's gaping mouth, the dog sees nothing. The bin man shouts. With purpose. Purpose. Come. Look. It's still alive.

The blue trousered people from the RSPCA excavate the dog from the rubbish heap. Tar is clumped around her eyes. The dog is all ribs and easy enough to lift between the two of them. One takes the hind legs, one takes the weight of the chest. The dog is young, in dog years barely a tween. They put a muzzle on the dog even though the dog is too weak to bite.

Come meet the dog. Boy nods. The dog is in the family room. There are two sofas and dog toys on the floor. There is a handler who introduces herself as Kirsty. She grins with all her teeth. She is pleased to meet you. Come meet the dog. The dog must meet every member of the family, in case the dog takes a dislike to one of you. Boy says: it's just me. The handler says: Oh good. Easy then. The dog is known for howling. She is known for curling her lips and snarling at men with beards. She is known for jumping up onto furniture as she does now, sitting proudly, bemused as the handler says: Get down. Get down. The handler looks at the boy and nods. The boy points at the ground too. The boy says: Come on, Dog.

Dog was from the countryside. That much was clear. Dog had numbers inked inside her ears. She was a dog for hunting, maybe, or for racing. A working animal, either way. Dog was from the countryside so Dog was afraid of cars. She did not understand roads, that they must be crossed, that cars sometimes do not stop for dogs. She had her bum bumped by a car more than once in her first month with Boy. Each time he let her off the lead she ran helter skelter beyond the railings of the park, beyond the yelling of Boy. Then the car would come. Dog on the zebra crossing, froze. The breaks slammed. The door opened. An argument. The driver's hand on their chest. Jesus Christ, ran right out into the road.

Boy took Dog to the countryside. There was a woodland that Boy liked and Dog liked it too. It smelt good. There was a smell of bodies in the woods, of living things and dead things. Boy loved the smell of the woods, but he smelt only moss and earth. Dog knew that in the woods the good smell is the smell of blood. When Dog came to the woods, she chased in circles, kicking up the dirt and shaking her head like she was rabid. She howled, howled, howled for joy. Dog and Boy came to the woods each weekend after that.

71

Once, dog came to the fireside with a deer's butchered hoof dangling from her mouth. The next weekend, Dog brought a partial jaw and for a moment Boy thought it was human. Dog dug and dug and brought out baby rabbits from the earth. Boy covered his mouth but Dog did not mean harm. Dog loved rabbits. Dog was a hunting dog, the boy thought. Strange that Dog was afraid of sheep, though. When the woolly devils came near, Dog prostrated herself in the dirt, or cowered, tail curled between her legs, and hid her face behind the boy. Boy did not, could not know that Bully had put her in a shed with two rams when she was only knee high. They had menaced their horns at the puppy while she quivered in the corner.

Boy decided that Dog was to be educated. Dog would learn how to sit, how to stay, how to heel, how to come here, now. Some things Dog already knew. Dog knew how to beg. Beg looked the same as love. Dog begged like it was missing Boy and Boy had left Dog all alone. Dog cried like it was mourning. Banshee Dog. Raven Dog. Dog yowled like death in the pub for crisps. Dog learnt to sit. For crisps. Dog learnt to sit when told. Dog did not learn to be quiet, come back, stay here, get down. Dog did not learn much. But what Dog knew, Dog knew. Dog knew your smell. Dog knew the glint men get in their eyes when they are drunk and picking for a fight. Dog knew that girlfriend was bad news and put her head between her paws and sighed. Dog knew how to mother.

Dog's belly was pink, spotted with grey and finely furred; Dog's hair had never grown back after Dog was spayed. Dog's nipples, redundant, milkless, occasionally flared red when Dog had fleas and scratched her belly too fiercely. Dog had a kitten. Kitten was orange too. Kitten staggered into the dog basket and stayed there, curled up, in the doggy stink. When bad news girlfriend put her things in boxes, she boxed the kitten up. Dog looked out of the window for days. Dog licked the walls until orange plaster came through. Dog licked her paws until the fur was all gone. Dog kept at it, licking the skin until the wound glistened and seethed.

See, Dog knew about love. Dog demanded love all the time. It was the furthest thing from slug slime. Dog begged: Place hands on me. Dog batted people with her paw until they placed hands on her. Dog knew about placing hands and how it heals. Dog liked the base of her tail, the sides of her thighs and the soft bit behind her ears to be scratched. Dog presented these spots to people with a wiggle, and nosed them hard with her thick skull when they did not oblige. Nose butting left, right, centre, in the ribs, the gut. Hard to have a conversation with Dog wanting to be loved all the time. The people grinned and put hands all over her, rubbing her hair all different ways so she was like a tumble dried dressing gown, puffed up and dropped on the floor. Their hands shirked around the swellings on her ribs.

Dog pulled on the lead when Boy walked her. She walked round the wrong side of a bollard and pulled Boy right over. A big wet graze on his knee. Jeans shredded and pockmarked with grit. His grip on the lead loosened and Dog bounded off, up the hill at full tilt past the emergency entrance of the hospital and into the shady park. Boy watched Dog getting smaller and smaller, skidding and baulking at the cars. The cars' emergency brakes screeched like night foxes. Boy on one knee now, ready to propose. His good knee working hard to lever him up, the bloody knee dragging behind. Boy's shoulders slump forward and his head hangs limp. Pain beats behind his eyes. Eyes stare after the speck of Dog; Dog slaloming through the park gates.

Dog wandered the park searching for squirrels. Kept looking over her shoulder for Boy, waiting for Boy to catch up. Squirrel scent everywhere. Spreading over the earth like mycelium. The stench of dead things. Goslings that didn't make it, pigeon feathers, mouse remains, a tiny white dog that pootles past her smelling richly of dead fleas. Dog feels the wind turn on her nose. She smells death on a young woman, so new a death, so fresh. Dog backs away. She hurries back to the gate, heads back across the road, waiting for cars to stop this time, and treading carefully. Dog finds Boy on his back. Dog noses at his armpits. So much sweat. Her eyes flick side to side, her brows twitching in their frown. Dog howls. Awoo. Awoo. Awoo. The sirens wail too. Awoo Awoo.

Walk home past the good pub. The doctors said don't drink until they know it's not a concussion, or something worse. Dog whining to be fed. Take that dog for pizza in the good pub. Have a half, just a half of ale. And a dog bowl. Dog's big pink tongue scooping the water out and sloshing it down her throat. Dog sits beside all the old and dying men like a patient ghost. She leans her slobbery jowls against their legs and their splayed hands come down from the heavens to rub her head. The old boys dribble some of their pints into the dog bowl and Dog laps them up gratefully. Dog will beg for crisps, for crusts, for the napkin in your hand to nose around the floor, to chew the grease stains out of. Dog will beg while you apologise to everyone and try to eat a pizza slice in two bites. Dog wanders to the end of the bar, and plops herself beside the painter with the handlebar moustache. Boy has one of the painter's watercolours on a wall in his bedroom. Autumn in the painting with leaves turning tangerine. The painter and Boy talk about the woods, about going to the woods to do some paintings. Boy tries to hide his excitement. Dog thumps her tail on the ground. Dog's ears pricked at the word 'woods'. Boy tells the painter he had funny turn that morning, out walking Dog. Dog whimpers and is stroked. She nuzzles her nose into the painter's knee. He strokes her and she whimpers and she keeps nudging at his leg. The painter fixes her with a look and Dog looks up. Incredulous. Boy apologises for disturbing the painter. They agree to find a date for the woods. Boy almost trips over Dog's tail. Mind your step. Dog whines as she is dragged away. See you soon, sire, Boy says. Dog barks and he tells her to be quiet. Four days later, the painter dies.

Dog knew. Always, Dog knew. Dog knew that he had been crying. When Boy had been crying, Dog was very good and did not beg for Boy's supper. Dog would come to rest her heavy skull upon his lap and gaze up at Boy through orange eyelashes. Dog stayed close by as Boy wandered round the house. Dog kept vigil outside the bathroom, followed Boy up the stairs, paused when Boy paused and leaned heavily on the bannister, watched Boy get dressed. Black trousers with a crease, black jacket with a western yoke, green shirt with pearl studs at the cuffs. Black trousers with stray dog hairs at the knees. Dog followed Boy back down the stairs, pressed her nose against the keyhole when Boy went out.

White service sheet. Autumn trees turning tangerine. Painter's cheeks daubed pink, a blush spot on the nose. Moustache waxed and eyes glued and hands arranged on his chest around a rosary. Sandwiches and pork pies eaten with hand covering mouth, trying to answer questions about how he knew him, whether they were close. Boy says the pub, and wishes he could say they worked together. Stink of dying flowers, stink of whisky, stink of worn out earth. Cling to him all as he walks home.

Boy didn't cry fat wet tears at the funeral but Dog knew that all the same Boy had wept. Thrown his fag stub on the ground and eye rolled heaven. Its splendid show of clouds. Trembled, then gave in, and Wept. Capital W like quivering lip and a mouth opening up to scream. Ow. No tears. Ow Ow. Banshee Boy. Raven Boy. Cawing on the road, all swathed in black.

Dog knew the smell of Boy when Boy had slept badly. Dog leapt into the bed and the mattress buckled like a cannon-balled pool. Dog lay beside him. Now beside him Dog's belly was moving gently, she bared it to him as an offering. She was submissive, front legs pulled up to her chest, and back legs splayed like a spatchcocked chicken, like a hamster on its back in the palm of a child, like a baby on a changing mat, like a lover, the dog's private parts were there, a streak of dampness and nothing else to indicate. This dog was yours. Dog trusted him entirely. Dog brought its love to him like a deer's rotting foot and left it, all gnawed and sticky with drool, at his feet, on his bed, buried among the blankets. Know this: Dog came to you when you were sick. Before you even knew.

The doctors thought it was something in his head. One day, Boy was having dinner and half his face stopped moving. Went slack. Latex mask-like slack. His left eye was open but the lid was soft. Couldn't blink. Water dribbled out of the left side of his lips and from his eyes, two tears slipped. He touched his face. Dog barked. Dog pushed her head against his side. Boy phoned an ambulance. He sounded drunk. The ambulance took a long time to come. Dog paced. Please calm down, old girl. Come here, Boy pleaded. Come on, Dog. Please come here. Dog came. Dog came and put her head on his feet and twitched her eyebrows. He put his hand on her chest. Time ticked by. Dog whimpered. Dog climbed onto the sofa and sat beside Boy like a wife. She put her head on his shoulder and looked out of the window. The ambulance was close. She wagged her tail and whined. She breathed near to his left ear and licked it once, twice. Boy swatted her away. She licked the ear again.

The doorbell rang. Dog ran to the door and sniffed at the gap to try and open it. Voices called through the letter flap. Sir, can you come to the door? Boy said yes. I think so. He walked to the door. One foot. Other foot. Dog ran up and down next to him. Nosed him on. At the door were people in green trousers. Dog knew this kind of people. She had met this kind before.

The people held Boy round his waist, and let him flop forward like a puppet. They walked him slowly down the stairs, and out into the road. They said well done. Dog trotted behind. Boy said go back inside. Go back inside. Dog whined. Boy was crying now. He lay down on a gurney and said I'm fine. One of the people took Dog by the collar and pulled her up the stairs. She twisted against the leather to see, but she did not bare her teeth. When they closed the door she howled. She jumped up on the sofa, pressed her paws and nose against the glass.

The people counted five signs that were not there, and said they were relieved. Boy looked relieved. Boy asked if they could wait a moment. He had called someone - to come look after the dog. From the window, Dog's eyebrows twitched.

Dog watched with distaste as Boy's bad news ex-girlfriend came. She put her hand over her mouth and her hand on his hand. Dog looked away. The lock clicked and Dog growled. She watched the ambulance doors close. She watched them drive her Boy away. Bad news ex-girlfriend said: Shh baby, shh, you're ok. Dog sniffed her, searching for Kitten. But no matter how hard Dog sniffed, that soft piss smell of cat was gone. Bad news ex-girlfriend sat down on the sofa and put her phone to her ear. So awful, she said it was, just so sad.

The hours passed. Like the hands on the clock, Dog spun round three times in her bed then lay down. She chewed her tail first. Afterwards, she licked her toes to pink.

The doctors thought it was something in Boy's head. But they checked and there was nothing there. No shadows on the images. No shapes. They took his temperature and made him urinate into a tube. The nurse put droppers of liquid into his eye. The liquid swilled over the eyeball, and still Boy could not blink. They put Boy on a drip. He hated needles like Dog hated beards. They took some blood and all the time they took it, Boy grizzled and yapped in pain. Boy's belly lurched. Boy wanted to be home. Boy cried. Boy could not hide his face. They took his temperature again. He said sorry, very sorry and they asked Boy just to wait.

The doctors thought it was something in Boy's head. But it was in the coiled mouse of his ear. A little nerve threading the legions of his face together had become inflamed. A sleeping virus, startled awake, the doctors explained.

Boy had had a flu for a long time, since the fall. Dog knew, Dog knew. Friends said he looked awful. Gaunt, like. Death, warmed up. Dog knew, Dog knew. Boy got hot in the night. Chattered his teeth. Soaked pillows through. Dog knew.

At the house, Dog watched bad news ex-girlfriend from a distance with suspicion and when she said good girl, Dog's ears ached. It was like slugs again, all over. Bad news ex-girlfriend went through all the drawers and cupboards. She flicked through notebooks and the fridge. She put on Boy's boxers and his t-shirt and got into Boy's bed. She starfished her legs so there was no space for Dog. Dog took the corner of the duvet and slowly pulled it onto the floor.

When Boy came home, next morning, all sinewy and thin, Dog span round in circles 'til she dizzied herself. He said: Not you, too. On his wrists he had two bracelets to tell him which way was up. Dog shook her head until her eyes were skew-whiffed and down was up and left was right and Dog was Boy and Boy was Dog. They giggled with the pleasure of each other. She licked his hands and proffered her belly. Dog held the laces of his shoes in her mouth for an hour til they were soaked through. Boy touched the walls to go up the stairs. Dog licked where he had touched.

The damage to a nerve from the infection can be severe. It may take many months to heal, sometimes even years. The face may not ever regain full animation. Your facial expressions may adapt so you may not recognise yourself for a time. Boy put cloth over the mirrors in the house, and tape over the camera on his laptop. He removed the cloth in the bathroom once a day and followed along a video of a woman saying letters very round and smiling and chewing and twitching her brows.

Boy lay in bed a lot, in the dark, while the virus passed through. Dog knew. Bad news ex-girlfriend rang and Boy looked at Dog and Dog looked at the floor and Boy did not pick up the phone. Dog lay with her face on his shoulder, on his chest, where the rash fizzed and she did not move until it went away.

One day, the painter's daughter phoned. Boy answered shyly. She asked him if he had any drawings by her father, squirrelled away. Boy said he did. He had a watercolour of trees turning tangerine in his bedroom: Would that do? She could come round to get it if she wanted. Just to take photographs, she said, then you can have it back. Boy said: Any time, he was always in. Dog knew.

When she came to the door, Dog barked to tell Boy to hurry up. Two yaps. Boy came shambling down the stairs in pyjamas, saying: Oi, don't be rude. Dog shrugged into the living room. Door opened. Dog heard Boy's voice and another voice making embarrassed and apologetic sounds that Dog approved of. People do not make these sounds enough. While the painter's daughter took down the picture and packed it away, Boy made tea. They chatted. She touched Dog with casual confidence, while she spoke. She held Dog between her legs and rubbed her chest and haunches and scruffed her head while looking at Boy, always at Boy. Dog sighed and let her tongue loll until drool coated the girl's hand. She did not mind. She wiped it on her trousers. They sipped their tea. Boy sat at an angle so she could not see his limp eye and cheek. Girl's hands rubbed and stroked and patted the swellings on Dog's ribs. She did not ask. She knew. Dog yawned loudly, showing all her teeth. Girl said she must be off. When Girl had gone, Boy thanked Dog for being sweet. Dog shrugged and nosed Boy back up to bed.

Girl came often after that. Girl watched Boy in the bathroom mirror. Girl trained Boy's muscles then: smile, frown, smile, frown. For their first walks outside, Girl took Dog's lead in case she pulled too hard for Boy. Dog did not pull. Then Boy took Dog's lead. They walked through the park, a little further every day. Dog learnt to heel. They sat in the good pub. Dog was fed crisps and stamped her feet with glee. Girl talked about the painter. Boy told Girl about the woods.

Girl drove them out to the woods. Girl thought it smelt good. There was a smell of bodies in the woods, of living things and dead things. Boy loved the smell of the woods, but he smelt only moss and earth. Girl said it smelt of rot, but in a good way. Dog scratched the earth and snorted. In the evening, Dog gnawed a bone by the fireside, while Girl and Boy spoke. Their knees touched. In the dark, Dog breathed and when she breathed, the space between her ribs ached. Come here, old Dog. Dog lay her head on his lap. Boy patted her ribs and they made a hollow sound in the quiet of the wood. Dog nosed between their knees and sat down heavily. She howled for joy. Girl howled too. Awoo. Awoo. That made Boy laugh and he joined in. Awoo Awoo Awoo.

They came to the woods each weekend after that.

The dog is in the ground now. In some ways it took a long time and in some ways it was quick. Boy did not really notice the long time. But he knew about the quick. Boy lay with Dog while the lumps grew. The lumps were made of Dog, and Boy would touch them. Dog would start at that; the heat of Boy's hands on the bruising bits of her body.

81

Her ears went first. A lump grew there, long and sticky, its skin kept oozing and scabbing. She could not hear Boy call her from across the park, or cars rushing down the road. Dog's ears were unhearing. Once Dog's ears heard all. Then a lump popped out of her armpit and she walked like a peg-legged sailor for a while, bumping into things and sitting down in the middle of the park. Then she panted and drooled all the time and whined at night. Dog licked round the edges of her dinner. Dog stopped begging for crisps. Dog brought no bones to the fire.

Boy lay with Dog while the candle on the vet's desk burned down and the poison moved around Dog, all riddled with welts of tissue growing where it ought not to. Dog was in the freezer for a long time until Boy could drive to the woods. Girl said she could drive, but Boy refused. She was his dog.

He dug a hole with a spade to slice through roots. Then he got inside the hole and scooped the earth with his hands like he was looking for rabbits. He pulled Dog's body into the hole beside him and he lay there for a while in the damp. He picked the slugs off Dog's thawing coat, some crystals still twinkling in the sun. Boy wept. He wept for all the time he had been thanking Dog, Dog was dying too. And all that time, Dog knew.

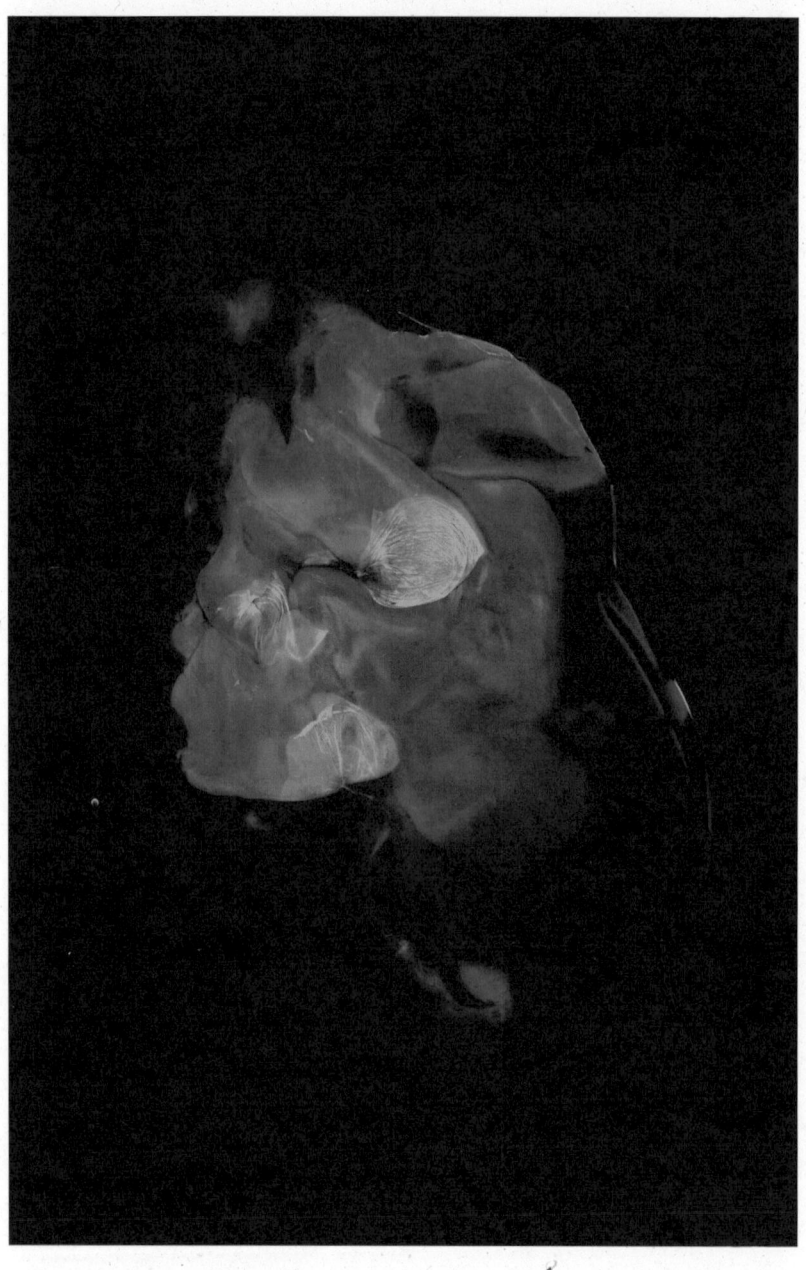

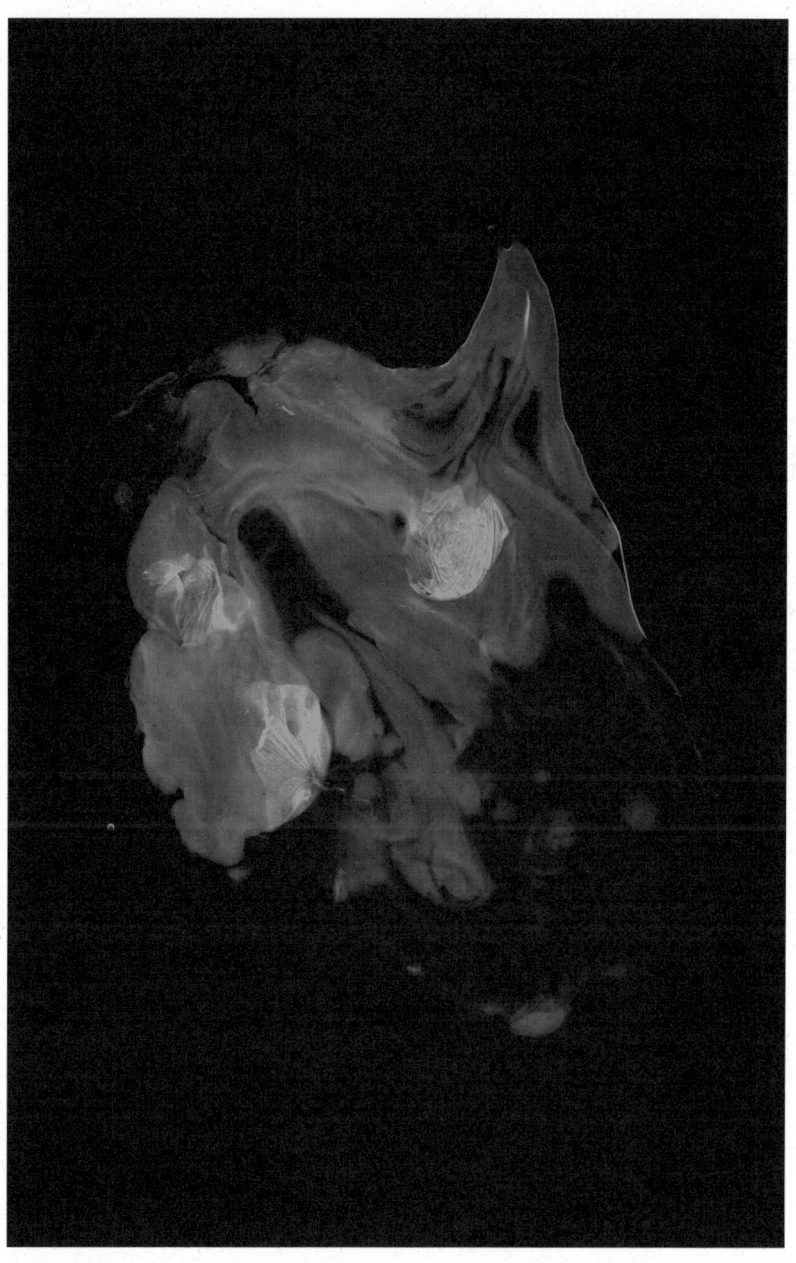

The Codfather

She was a creature of such loveliness that he couldn't bear
to walk past the window without stopping to look through
the glass. The window faced right out onto the street and all
day people walked by, pushing their prams and squawking
into their phones, their eyes casting over the display. None
of them saw her. Often they thought the shop was empty
or closed, her impeccable stillness shielding her from their
brisk sight. If she was in with her head bowed over her book
at the counter and her hair falling over her shoulders, and
not the other bookseller, who was a man, there was nothing
he could do but push open the door. The bell rang, and her
head lifted. Then they were together in the shop. The fibres
of her white cardigan lilted in the breeze and her perfume
gusted suggestively towards him, dragged there by the
closing door. He stepped forwards to ask her how she was.
He was greeted by her great big eyes open in recognition.
Her mouth opened to reply. Her resolve melting away as the
obligation of his presence on this side of the glass pressed
hotly against her.

"They're good guys," her father said as they walked side by side
back to the house, her father closest to the curb, passing the
bag of chips between them. She looked back over her shoulder,
through the chip shop window, to the heavy set men, their
T-shirts stretched like cling film over their bellies, sinking
cages into puckering oil. They handled their business silently.
No need for the word 'Vinegar?' when the bottle is tipped and

bristling, a drip forming at its nib and threatening to give. "Yes, please, more," she had said. Then the bottle was shaken like a tambourine, leaving acrid notes stinging in the air. The vinegar made her face feel pointy as she sank her teeth into another sodden chip. Her father barely winced. "You should take their number for emergencies. They'd sort it out." When the chippy's matriarch died, her coffin was attended by men in dark glasses and a horse drawn hearse moved glacially along the high street, decked out with flowers. Maureen was a pillar of the community, and now her three sons were too. As a little girl, she had loved them for the golden shards of batter they had slipped into her sticky fingers. Her father had left her there, when he'd had urgent business to attend to, and she had sat on the counter, swinging her legs and chatting gibberish. Now she understood better what 'sorting out' meant, and regarded the middle aged sons' hands with uneasy reverence as they squeezed ketchup bottles and shovelled chips into bags.

It was the end of her first day. Her father had pretended he was just passing and hadn't planned to pick her up, but she had seen him waiting on the corner. He had stood there for half an hour, his eyes scanning the road.

"What kind of emergencies?"

"Junkies, after the till," he offered. She swatted away this suggestion; they hardly carried any cash these days. Her father looked at her, and sighed, "You know what I'm saying." There were things even he wasn't brave enough to name.

Later, in the privacy of her childhood bedroom, surrounded by boxes, she met the spectre of her tired eyes in the window. She placed her own fingers on her collar bone, where the bruise was yellowing. She pulled her phone from her pocket and found the text her father had sent her. "Rick says anything happens, text him and they'll come round." She saved the attached number, the red emergency asterix pinning 'The Codfather*' to the top of her contacts.

Her father had been worried that it would be too much for her to start working, so soon after the break up (he called it the "— break up", with the same distinct hesitation every time), but she found it a welcome distraction. In fact, she was a natural. Bookselling was mostly about making people believe that you liked the same things they did, and she had always been good at that. With a little encouragement, the customers shared precise details about their grannies and mothers and wives so that she could produce a book with a blurb so resonant they'd beam and lavish her with thanks. She enjoyed the cursory flirtation that thrummed between her and the young men who came in looking for new poetry. She stood on tiptoes to fish an anthology down from the top shelf, her t-shirt lifting away from her waistband to expose a crescent of taut flesh. Her mouth a bow around the closing sentence; "This is one of my favourites," she lied. It worked every time. Scan it out, punch it in, tap their card and it was over. Now she was not on social media (she'd had to close down her accounts) she wondered if this was how people met in real life, but the young men never returned, or, if they did, she didn't recognise them. For the minutes they were with her, she adored them, and then they were gone. In the end, it was a relief.

She greeted him as any other customer, with a smile. He was older, greying, self conscious in his crisp jeans. She nodded placidly while he described the highs and lows of the last week, and felt genuinely pleased when he said the shop had a good poetry section (she had ordered in new stock that week). He asked her what she was reading at the moment and she walked him to a pile of shiny hardbacks that she was keen to shift. He bought one, obediently. He came in again the following Tuesday. And the one after that. They talked about his new fitness regime, the weather, and current bestsellers. If he asked her about herself, she gave a delphic reply. He asked her where she lived, and she told him: "I grew up round here." There were no follow up questions. He grew up in Ealing, did she know it? "I think I've been." Each Tuesday she waited for the conversation to dry up, her fingers stroking the passing seconds on her throat. He always bought a book before he left.

She felt the prickle of his eyes on her before the bell rang.
"If you were to compare anyone to W. G. Sebald, who would it be?" She hated it when he tested her intellect like this. Though she had no interest in impressing him, the part of her that could not bear to be found wanting, that same part that easily lied that she had seen a film only to excuse herself and read the synopsis in the loo, was provoked and she found herself flitting about the shelves pulling doomish European writers out to present to him like a puffed up bird.

He hovered a foot back from the counter, blocking the narrow gangway to the cluttered backroom, and turned each book over in his hands, running his fingers over the spines and reading the blurbs in the silence. The words might as well have been hieroglyphs. It was important to seem thoughtful, indecisive. He needed to delay the inevitable transaction, which marked the end of their encounter. She dropped her eyes to her own book, though she could not find her place again. Her ribs tickled and her nipples hardened with the chill of his extended companionship. Surreptitiously, she extracted her phone from her pocket and laid it on the counter top, unlocked. His visits were the only time that she wished the shop was busy. In the lull of a January Tuesday, he latched onto her with ease.

She had watched many first dates unfold in the shop. Always the man led the woman around the shop, showing her first the books that he had read and found derivative, and then filling her hands with books that had changed him, like a magpie decorates a nest. She pondered if he was younger and better looking, whether she would have been flattered by his visits and let him lead her around too. She worried that her discomfort meant that she was superficial. Out of the corner of her eye, she noticed that his shoes were supremely polished. She wondered, not for the first time, what he did for money.

The bell rang again. A woman with a pram cajoled a toddler to walk ahead.
"Hello, how are you?" The woman smiled politely and parked the pram by the sticker books. "Do you need any help?" she asked and hoped the woman would say yes.
"No, no thank you. We won't be long."
"Please, take your time," she said, and meant it.

She had beautiful manners. They gave her an old fashioned quality that made him want to take her hand. He retreated to the backroom to think about her amongst the cookbooks. The bell tinkled again. Heavily he realised that they would never be uninterrupted, here. He would leave the shop deflated, the good mood that his early run had ignited, snuffed by her strangeness. What was her name? How old was she? If he asked, surely she would tell him. How could she not. But how could he ask with all these interlopers in earshot, sharing the intimacy that he alone had been brave enough to request. He sat on the carpeted ground, and opened one of the books she had given him, trailing his fingers over the smooth paper. He wondered how to ask her out. But then why would he ask her out, when there was something lovely about her perched on that tall chair, surrounded by books, smiling at toddlers and slipping thin volumes into tight gaps. He shuddered with pleasure to think of being asked to stay after closing. To be hidden there with her as the shutters came down.

"Have a nice day! I hope he likes it," she chirruped as the door swung shut. Uneasily, she rose from her chair. Her bladder ached. The bathroom was through the backroom, through a door hidden there. She bounced from foot to foot, sucked in her stomach. There was no more time.

"I'm just nipping to the loo," her eyes closed as she scurried through the backroom, almost tripping over his shiny shoes. He got clumsily to his feet, brushed himself down. Her hand gripped the doorknob, as his voice behind her declared: "These two are very good. I think I'll get them." Her head winched over her shoulder. Her cheeks flushed. She smiled. He smiled back. Her teeth squeaked against themselves.

In the acerbic light of the loo, the door locked, she let out a gasp as her bladder emptied. She clamped her hand to her throat and squeezed her eyes shut and prayed he hadn't heard. She imagined his ear pressed up against the door. She squeezed the thought from her brain. Normal people didn't do that. A minute elapsed. She sat there, with her knickers round her ankles, and tugged at a loose string protruding from the seam on the cuff of her cardigan. The longer she sat there, the worse it would be to face him again. She flushed, which rattled the pipes tremendously, and hoped he'd scurry away like a rat when the lights came on. And when she unlocked the door, and poked her head out, and found the shop empty, she gasped again.

She returned to her chair and found there the books abandoned in a haphazard pile on the seat.

-

Two weeks passed without him. She stopped expecting him. There were other regulars, as native to bookshops as they are to pubs. She got to know them and love them. She gladly gave Ruth her email so she could send her some poetry. She felt touched when Douglas showed her some of his most recent cob web paintings and she agreed he had captured the frost well. Some of them knew her father, so they asked her how long she had been back home. She told them she had been back since graduation, which was almost true. Each day, the shutters came up, came down, and she walked home, alone. She started to enjoy it, being alone. She stared less and less at her reflection in the window. The bruise disappeared. Slowly she unpacked her boxes, slotted her own books onto shelves. The shop manager congratulated her on the spike in poetry sales. She brought home chips to her father, and found he was not waiting for her in the kitchen.

Through the window, he watched her giggle, her hands shimmering the air, and wondered what had possessed her to engage in such animated conversation with this other man. His cheeks burned. He pushed the door with such force that one of the window display books fell over. It had been balanced upright on its splayed pages, now it was lying face down, snapped shut.

He righted the book, gingerly. She thanked him with a nod, her eyes stuck to him for a moment too long. Her heart throbbed. She could hear it pulsing in her skull. It was the same feeling she had that night, her last night at the pub, when she had gone into the office to change her top after a Guinness was spilt on her. The lock hadn't clicked properly. She had told him that it could never happen at work, even if they were on the same shift. She had used the wet t-shirt to wipe him off her back afterwards.

She snapped her focus back to her current customer, locking her eyes with his. He was tall, with full lips, crested with stubble. He exuded gentleness. She noticed fondly his sloping shoulders and scuffed trainers. She slid the book into a paper bag and taped it closed. Passing it to him, she said she hoped he liked it, and meant it.

"Really, she's one of my favourite writers -" still holding it, "Strange but so, so good."

"I'm looking forward to it." He beamed with real warmth as he tucked the book under his arm and extended his hand. "It was nice to meet you, Lydia." Still lingering by the door, his neck prickled as he said it. As the stranger turned to leave, he met him, chest to chest.

"What did you get?" he asked curtly. The stranger looked down at him in surprise and answered. The title didn't matter much. He'd read it was the main thing. "I never got on with her. I find her prose verbose." He directed the criticism at Lydia, who began to shuffle the pencils in the pot in front of her.

"I'll bear that in mind." Unruffled, the stranger sidestepped round him, and slipped out onto the street. He kept his eyes trained on the stranger until he disappeared beyond the frame of the window.

"Who was that?" He came around to the open side of the counter, where he could see her dangling feet. She shrugged.

"He comes in quite a lot." She had never seen him before but as she hoped it would turn the screw.

"Lydia is a nice name." His eyes were hard. "Do you know what it means?"

"'Noble one.'" Her voice was curt.

"Yes. Or beautiful." He fanned his hand in the air, "There are different interpretations." She nodded, swallowing the spit that was pooling in her mouth. She watched him lift a Mother's Day card from the spinning rack by her shoulder. "Are you named after someone?" He put it back.

"My mum just liked it," she snapped. She was not disguising her impatience well enough, reminding herself that she was at work. Then: "She was going to call me Lewis, if I was a boy." He shook his head slowly, seeming to savour the surprise of this new information, freely given. A smile tugged at his lips and she shivered. The way he was swirling her name on his tongue made her stomach roll.

"I'll just have a browse, if you excuse me, Lydia."

The other customers left, one by one. When they were alone, he came back to the counter and laid a book upon it. She took it. He rested his elbows on the counter and said, slowly: "Very good things started to happen for me, after I came in here." She nodded, waving the book hopelessly in front of the scanner. It wouldn't scan. She turned it over and after some clicks of the mouse began to type the code in as he told her: "All the reading, meeting likeminded people, young, intelligent people." She raised her eyebrows and tapped the price into the till, the red numbers changing. "I've got the time now. The happiest times in my life -" he paused, for emphasis, "Have been the months after a relationship has come to an end."

"That's interesting," she said flatly. She had always suspected he was divorced. Then, spurred by a sudden desire to make him squirm, she added: "I've always felt break ups were very revealing. You can tell a lot by how well a person grieves."

"Are you someone who likes to dwell on the past?"

"Everyone is," she said, simply. "You either recognise that, or you're someone who spends their life looking for distractions." The implication seethed between them. She could not bring herself to meet his eyes. She felt them, on her scalp, frisking her for an explanation. The itch of duty rose around her ears. She pulled at the cardigan wool, which suddenly gave, unravelling in a delightful wiggle. She would not apologise. She swivelled on her chair to face him. "That's ten ninety nine please." Holding the card machine up to him like a knife. "Would you like a receipt?"

-

His grip tightened around her wrist.

A subtle inflection of his head. Somewhere between tapping his card and grabbing her, he had asked her a question. Now he was waiting. She wriggled her hand but he wouldn't budge. "I don't know."

"Think," he said. So she thought. All of her politeness and her smiles snagged inside her. Her collar bone itched.

"Can you repeat -" and before she got the question out, he did, more tersely -

"Are you free on the thirteenth?"

"I have to check my calendar," she hissed, yanking her hand free.

Fingers shaking, she took out her phone. His hand knocked rigidly against his thigh as he watched her studying the screen. He noticed how red the skin on her wrist was. He shouldn't have grabbed her. He felt ashamed. But he would make it up to her. He had to. Yes, she had forced his hand. Her evasiveness. The insult of her lies, each one of them, to undermine him, to undermine the connection that he knew they shared. And she had wounded him, intentionally. It was just a reflex, to get her to listen to him. But all the same, he had let himself down. So he would make it up to her. When they were alone, and - he glanced towards the door - far away from this panopticon, he would make her know how sorry he was.

She put her phone down and looked up at him, and smiled. She didn't need to check her calendar to know that she was not free; the thirteenth of March was her birthday. She was going to be twenty-two. She thought about telling him what was about to happen, but then she did not know herself.

"Well?" he pressed. Her eyes found their way past him to the window and the faces there that looked back.

"Well what?" The bell rang and he turned to see who was there.

-

She sat on a chair in the empty chip shop, fiddling with the frayed cuff of her cardigan. Her father was on his way. She gazed straight ahead, through the display glass, to the battered sausages basking in the golden light.

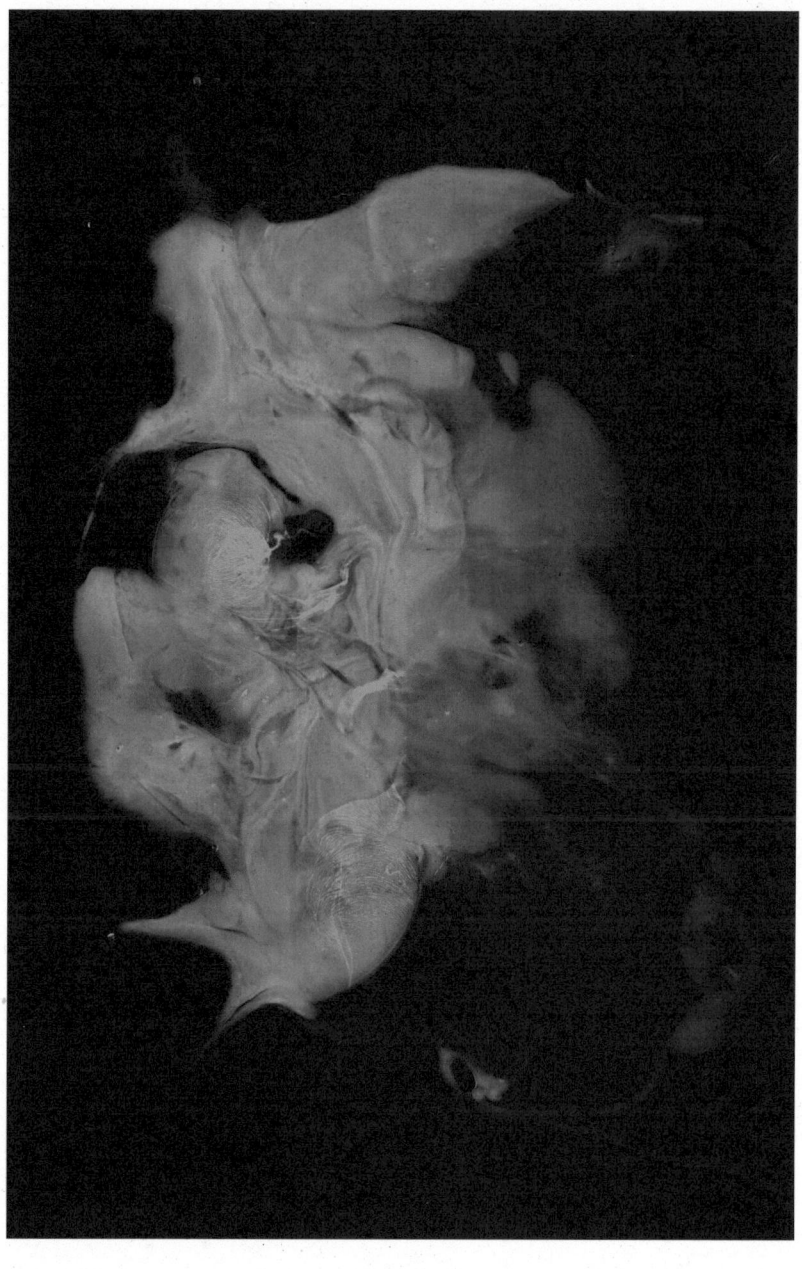

Thin Soup

We arrive at the house in the beetle-dark, silently retrieving the key from under a plant pot and removing our shoes to soften our steps. We climb into the bed, made up in the guest room, and swaddle ourselves in the stiff, cold sheets. I rub my icy feet against Matthew's thighs, which are always hot as fresh loaves. It is the end of December, almost Christmas.

In the morning, I lean over the side of the bed, groping in the tangle of yesterday's clothes for my phone. I see my breath billow as I groan. The blood rushes to my head and I feel dizzy when I lurch myself upright. I check the time - early. I curl back into him. He is still soft with sleep and whimpers with pleasure as my arms slip round him, pulling his warm back close against my belly. I close my eyes. The thought comes: she is dying.

I dress quickly. Everything is the same as yesterday, even my underwear. In the mirror in the bathroom, with bobby pins and a hair band gripped between my teeth, I french plait my hair, tucking the last wisps behind my ears. When I was young, my mother used to braid my hair so tightly I could hardly blink.

In the kitchen, Andrea is sitting at the table, nursing a coffee and making notes in biro around a crossword. She looks up. My sister is older than me by ten years. She is the picture of our mother: thin nose, dimples like stapled fabric, a downturned mouth. I take after my father. His softness, his ruddiness, his big seal eyes.

"Was the journey okay?" Andrea asks, her eyes dropping back to the crossword.

"No issues."

"Was it easy to get a taxi from the station? I would have picked you up, only I'd been up since five."

Her alarm must have woken me this morning, I think, mustering the patience to reply:

"It was all very straightforward," Andrea raises an eyebrow, perhaps at a difficult clue, "we were shattered too."

"So you slept well?" I push thoughts of the ice ferns on the window aside.

"Yes, fine. You?" Andrea sighs. The sigh whistles on as she folds the paper up, and clips it closed with her biro.

"We'll go and see her today." I open the lid of the coffee pot on the stove, to see if there is any left. Only the last dregs, rapidly evaporating. Andrea unclips the biro and unfolds the paper. She inquires, scratching away, "Is Matthew ready?"

Matthew, still bleary, drives in silence. Andrea sits in the passenger seat, wincing. She tells him to be careful of the wing mirrors at every blind corner. He pulls up outside the hospital. I squeeze his shoulder as I climb out. Andrea recites the shopping list again and Matthew nods at every item. He pulls the door closed, and she stops him, holding it.

"Nice crackers," she reiterates, "not the cheap ones." Matthew looks at me and I smile with the side of my mouth.

In her convalescence, my mother has become an ugly medieval angel, suffering for our sins. Her cheeks are caving in around her mouth; her dentures sitting in water on the bedside table. She is propped up on pillows, with a hospital blanket tucked right up under her chin. Surrounded by monitors, and limp Christmas decorations, it makes a disturbing tableau.

My mother beckons me closer with a gnarled finger. Emaciation has thrown her knuckles into shocking protrusion like the knots in a tree. Her wedding ring and engagement ring knock together, sliding up and down. My mother's hands were always beautiful. Lavishly moisturised, with carefully filed, soft pink crescents for nails. Now those nails are ridged and square. I take a very small step towards the bed, and take her papery hand. When she breathes, her lungs make a whistling sound.

"They put me in this geriatric ward. It's not right," she squeezes my hand. "They're all gone," with her other hand she taps her temple, "in there."

The temple hand lifts from her face and gropes around in the air for mine, which I bring closer to her. Finding my chin, she clutches it. She turns my head this way and that. "You've put on weight."

"Probably." I stopped disputing my mother's aesthetic observations years ago. I once presented her with a chart detailing my never fluctuating weight over two months and she simply replied that there was a difference between weight and fat. She fondles a frond of hair that has come loose from behind my ear.

"You shouldn't wear your hair like this. It looks thin." I let go of her hand.

"*Mummy*," Andrea scolds her gently as she guides me out of the way to stand by the window. My sister proceeds to ask our mother a series of questions about meals and pillows. Our mother rolls her head back and lets her chin hang open slightly, in perfect mimicry of a corpse.

"Blood from a stone," Andrea mutters as we close the curtain round our mother, who has a sudden headache. She has requested more morphine, and to be left alone. Andrea marches off in search of a nurse. I drift along after her, but she snaps round, fixing me with a hypodermic look. She sends me away to get two cups of tea from the Costa by the reception.

I wait in the queue behind three doctors in scrubs. My wisdom tooth is playing up today. It has never fully emerged and the loose flap of gum that covers it sometimes swells up and blisters. I remember when my first tooth got wobbly. When my mother wasn't looking, I'd wiggle it with my tongue and feel the little hot squirt of blood issue from under it. I push my tongue under the gum flap now as subtly as I can, and wiggle it to comfort myself. The tea is weak and boiling. I slosh it into the back of my mouth, where it might cauterise the wound I have worried into redness.

Andrea is sitting on the floor when I turn the corner into the ward. She is leaning against the wall, fanning herself with a leaflet. She has unbuttoned her blouse to expose the shocking pink of her clavicle.

"Hot flush", she explains as I lower myself down beside her and push the paper cup of tea against her foot. She turns to look at me. "*Mummy is dying.*" I sip my tea. It scalds my throat as I swallow. I can track its path down my oesophagus and into my belly by the pain. I take Andrea's hand in mine.

"What did the nurse say?" Andrea withdraws her hand from mine and whirls it in the air.

"Waiting on tests, waiting on bloods, surgery, no surgery, either way," Andrea's hand stops twirling to form the bunny ears of ennui. Her fingers twitch, "risks." I test the tea again with my tongue. "They said she hasn't been eating."

"Well, she's probably worried about getting fat." My sister

laughs. We sit in contented silence for a moment before levering ourselves onto our feet.

Our mother began complaining of a bellyache a month ago. She has suffered with her gut for some time. I can track the last fifteen years of our relationship by the phone calls I've received in which my mother has detailed the causes and symptoms of her food poisoning. Andrea and I are probably guilty of hastening our mother's death with our incredulity.

Matthew picks us up at midday. When we get back, I leave him and Andrea in the kitchen. My husband by the stove, stirring a large pan of risotto, and my sister making nervous noises around him, wiping the surfaces continually. I climb onto the bed, lean my head against the cold metal headboard, and close my eyes. My stomach throbs in its familiar way.

Like my mother, I am often sick. When I was too old to be rocked to sleep but not old enough to fend for myself, my mother stopped disguising how taxing she found my illnesses. She hated being summoned from work to the school reception to collect her waif. My father never came. She'd arrange me on the back seat, sigh, and say, "Why he can't pick you up is beyond me," the same way every time.

When we got home, she would put me in her own bed. It was always laid with white sheets. Over their egg white peaks, like a turbulent sea, hazy apparitions of teddies would rise and fall on their waves. Nursery rhyme characters with tootling flutes would weave their drunken, merry way along the bookshelves and plop into my sick bowl. I remember Andrea sitting at the end of the bed. Only she must have been at university by then, meeting Ian, so that can't be right. All night I'd writhe, twisting the sheets into ropes, clutching my stomach, making the rumbling, whimpering sounds of a dying animal.

If it was a bad one, my mother clucked with worry around me and brought me thin soups and Rennie's tablets. Those fat pellets of chalk made no difference except turning my choked-up bile into a pale, minty froth.

Once, the doctor came and told her it was probably nerves. He prescribed a diet of plain crackers, water (sipped), and rest. Dissatisfied with this diagnosis, I convinced myself that I had been poisoned by a black speck in a piece of fish I'd been served at school dinners. The shadow had disturbed me and I had probed the fish finger with my fork until it resembled cat food. I'm not sure, now that I think about it, that I ate even a single mouthful but I refused to eat school lunch again after that. To evade the bionic gaze of the dinner ladies, I cut my food up very small and moved it around the plate. Later I learned to syphon some of it into my water cup and carry this over to the water dispenser, which was right beside the bin. Little by little, the uneaten lunch would diminish, and I would be permitted to exit the hall.

Matthew has turned on the radio, loud enough to override Andrea's wittering. I take several deep breaths and two strong painkillers. I place both my palms on the table, breathing into the pain in my gut. Andrea is polishing cutlery with a red tea towel. I lower myself into a chair. Matthew turns to face me, his eyes occasionally drifting back to the pan of bubbling rice. He dries his hands on his jeans.

"You'll feel better after eating." Over the years his patience has worn thin. He used to make me describe the pain, while he googled symptoms and prodded his own belly. He'd make me large mugs of ginger tea, run deep baths, crack pills out of the packet and hand them to me. Now he suspects, having lived with me for almost three decades, that my stomach aches are at best psychosomatic and, at worst, self-inflicted. I regard the hot creamy rice thickening behind him. Sensing my agony, he adds, "Just have a little bit. Then you can go to bed."

Andrea eats methodically, working her way into the centre of her plate from the edges. Her knife and fork work in discreet union to ensure that every mouthful is tidily constructed and directed into her mouth. Not a grain is missed. Matthew eats with his fork upturned "like a shovel". He is also guilty of brandishing his cutlery when telling a story, slashing his knife in the air for emphasis. My mother disapproves of his table manners, and his stories. I've always liked both. He pushes back from the table when he is finished, legs outstretched and rests his hands on his stomach. His plate scraped, his cutlery sucked clean and slung onto his scrunched napkin. Andrea lines hers up and smooths her napkin flat. I gingerly place my fork on the edge of the plate. I haven't used my knife. My risotto is spread about in a lumpen archipelago. Matthew raises an eyebrow at me and I scoop one of the islands into my mouth. He nods. I place my fork down again and say I'm off to bed. Matthew smiles over the crest of his full belly. He looks like my father when he sits like this - digesting. Happy as a pig in shit.

Unlike Matthew, my father was an awful cook. Still, the man could eat. In the early days following the divorce, before he met Sandra, he didn't even own a fridge. He'd always take me to the caff for ham, egg and chips. Breakfast or dinner, the same. I'd have a dicky belly when I came home, and need to stay in bed for several days. My mother would ring round her friends, all of whom would be too busy to take care of me. Then she'd throw her head to the ceiling and ask God "Why?"

The divorce mostly played out like this. My mother, stoically enduring. My mother, carefully inventorying her sacrifices so she could whip them out at any time. My mother phoning Andrea, who always answered. My mother phoning my father, who never did. My mother, making me a plate of cucumber sticks. My mother, measuring my waist and frowning. My mother, rushing upstairs to change into a shorter dress when she heard the revving of my father's car in the drive. My father, revving in the driveway, cigarette dangling from his lips. My father, ignoring every rule my mother set. My father, arriving late to get me from school, never arriving at all, leaving me with friends while he went out. My father, taking me to parties. My father, feeding me crisps and cheese and bread.

When they were together, their arguments always erupted from the kitchen. The door slamming shut behind my father as he wiped sauce off his lapel. The kitchen was my mother's realm. She paced the galley of it like a tiger, peeler gripped in her fist. I sat on the stairs and listened. Whump. My mother threw a whole roast chicken at his head, once. Then he left, for the final time, and the house was quiet. The grease stain where the chicken had slid down the wall remained. Even after it was repainted, the colour was never the same. In his wake, the house smelt of bleach, mostly, and Ajax, an acidic scouring powder that left a red ring round my mother's forearms, just above where her marigolds stretched. My mother and I only had cold suppers after that, to save on washing up.

Andrea and I visit the hospital again the following day. Our mother is asleep when we arrive. The nurse explains that she hasn't eaten for seven days. This is the end now. She will drift in and out. As if she has been listening all the time, my mother's eyes spring open. She waves the nurse away and asks suspiciously if anyone else is coming to see her. She makes a few grumbling remarks about the thanklessness of motherhood. I suggest that Matthew might pop in.

"That man," she groans.

"Ian is dropping the girls over later." I notice that every time Andrea says her ex-husband's name, she uses a teetering sing-song voice, with an upward inflection. The kind of sunny voice used by nurses just before they shove a speculum into your vagina. Ian is, after all, a mild embarrassment. But Ian is not Matthew, and the girls are the girls, so our mother's concrete complexion brightens.

Ian is an insurance broker. He is earnest and polite. He always wears hiking shoes on the weekend, even when he is only going to the supermarket. When they were young and amorous, Ian faithfully encouraged Andrea to search for her real dad, suggesting that it would be special if her father - a stranger - could walk her down the aisle. Andrea found her father in the South of France. It only took one brief phone call. He was still working on his pots and sketching his silk-draped wife in the very same studio that our mother had visited in the 60s. Andrea found him wholly unsatisfactory. He was not invited to the wedding.

Instead, our mother gave Andrea away. She handed her first daughter's open palm to Ian like the last chocolate in the box. It helped that Ian was wealthy, of course, and that Andrea desperately wanted children. It particularly helped that Ian was grateful; Matthew would never learn that lesson. After their first dance was over, Ian slipped away to talk earnestly to his best man. Matthew and I spun my sister around all night. Matthew even waltzed my mother round the floor, and I caught her, just once, with her head thrown back in delight. Ian and Andrea divorced ten years later.

Andrea's daughters come in the late afternoon. Amy is finishing her GCSEs and Suzie is at university now, first year. They are easily slim, willow-limbed, their tiny nipples pushing through thin vests in the chill of the ward. My mother's eyes light up. She reaches out her hands to hold them and they look at each other before taking a hand each, squeezing and leaning in to receive a kiss on their firm cheeks. She sinks back into her pillows in bliss. "Stunning girls," she smiles at them, gushingly, "becoming such beauties." They cross their arms over their chests and blush. My eyes ache a little. Andrea looks over at me. I brave a smile. She says the girls have plans.

"Nice to see you, granny,"

"Please don't call me that - so ageing," she is frail as a skeleton piped from meringue. The girls smile, kiss their mother, tug on their hoodies and go. My own mother can't hide her disappointment.

"They are so pretty," she beams at Andrea, "I don't know why they have to dress like boys."

I was younger than Suzie the day that I moved out. I'll never forget the look my mother gave me when I came down in baggy jeans and a felted jumper that pressed my breasts flat. My hair hacked short. I had a rucksack on one shoulder and a carpet bag stuffed full of books. I was fucking off, I said, in no uncertain terms, and I would not be back. She waited by the door, wringing a dishcloth in her hands. Matthew had a bedsit in Forest Hill, near Dad's. Matthew had a hot plate and trangia for boiling water. He made omelettes that leaked lakes of butter into chipped plates and he swabbed them clean with thick hunks of bread. We ate in bed. Perhaps the second time we slept together, I asked him if he had a tape measure so I could check the circumference of my thighs. He told me he didn't have one. I asked to move in. I was almost eighteen. When I told my mother, she said, "Fine. Just don't get pregnant." I rolled my eyes, hand on the latch. She snarled, "You're the kind of girl -" a pause like a snake tasting the air, "that a baby would make fat."

When we get back from the hospital, I go straight to bed and Matthew doesn't try to stop me. I think he looks tired. Andrea hovers by the bedroom door for a moment. She breathes in, meets my eye, and then closes the door quietly with a sigh. I lie in bed, holding my stomach, and listen to their suppressed conversation. I hear my name once or twice. Matthew has only ever wished there was more of me. That, and a baby, are the only things I haven't given him. As the thought lingers, sleep seeps in to quell it. For these few hours, every night, I am not hungry. This is how I understand mercy.

When I was seventeen, I was invited to spend Christmas with my father. Sandra had bought a turkey from Harrod's. They were living in London by then. My mother had served sandwiches for two years, made with cold ham that Andrea brought over. I got the train up and my father met me at Victoria Station. We stayed up late, in the kitchen, talking over coffee. He had a splash in his, 'a livener'. He offered me one and I declined. Before bed, he made me toast with lashings of butter and hot chocolate. Without asking this time, he tipped his hip-flask into my cup. For a growing girl, he said. I bristled. Then took a sip.

What I remember most of that Christmas is the smell of sizzling turkey skin, nutmegged bread sauce, and mulled wine coming up through the floorboards, and the rich gravy of inebriated chatter, booming away.

In my father's study above the party, I was lying floppy and febrile in the camp bed that was quickly constructed for me. I had woken with my habitual stomach cramps. Rushing down the steep wooden stairs to get to the toilet, I fainted. My tumbling corpse hit the bannister, splitting one of the thin, turned spokes, which snapped savagely round my thigh. At the bottom of the stairs I lay, shaking. My skull rattled. I heard the rush of a train hissing along its rails, and then my father's voice, calling my name.

He laid me out in bed, tucked me in, and called my mother. Now I was curled up, shivering, waiting for her to arrive. She put my arm over her shoulder and walked me, still smocked with blankets, out to the street. Down the stairs, one at a time, her small frame trembling under the weight of my bones. She folded me neatly into the back of the car. From her handbag she produced a flask, unscrewed the top and handed it to me. "Soup," she said, "not very festive, but it will do."

The guest room is freezing when I wake up, though Matthew is sleeping soundly. I check my phone, squinting at the bright screen. It is the middle of the night. My stomach squelches round itself. I pick my way to the bathroom, bend myself over the loo and let my sour spit dribble out. Crumpled on the tiles, I close my eyes. I imagine my mother in her hospital bed, her own intestines shrivelling. Aching, prickling with hunger. I jerk myself awake.

I switch on the pelmet lights in the kitchen. I open the cupboard, the humming fridge, drag out a big pot and fill it with water. A stock cube, roughly cut veg, the end of a lump of parmesan. I make soup for my mother in the middle of the night. I use a masher to break the potatoes up. Watch it simmer under the glass lid. I pour it into a flask, splashing some on the marble surfaces. I do not wipe it up. There, it coagulates, crusts like blood. I get in the car, wearing my pyjamas, and Andrea's posh clogs. I take it to her.

When I get to the hospital, the sky is mauve and spread thinly with clouds like cottage cheese. I slip through the automatic doors. The reception is empty, a coffee cup abandoned on the desk. I take the lift up. Three floors. The corridors are stiffly lit and strung with limp tinsel. The ward itself is sleepy dark. The machines around her bed flicker, blue, green, red. She is unconscious. Her mouth slack. Her eyelids relaxed and wrinkleless. I sit with her for a while. After an hour, I can feel my own eyelids drooping. I pour myself a capful of the soup and sip it. It is warm in my stomach, radiating out to my blue fingers, my purple toes. I draw my feet up onto the chair and tuck my knees under my chin. I pour myself another capful. Then another. My mother does not stir. Not a single flexing of a finger, not a hair. The monitors mark the slowing of her heart. I watch the tendon in her throat contract, and her head droop more heavily to the side.

When the flask is empty, I stand up, leave the room, and inform the duty nurse that my mother has died.

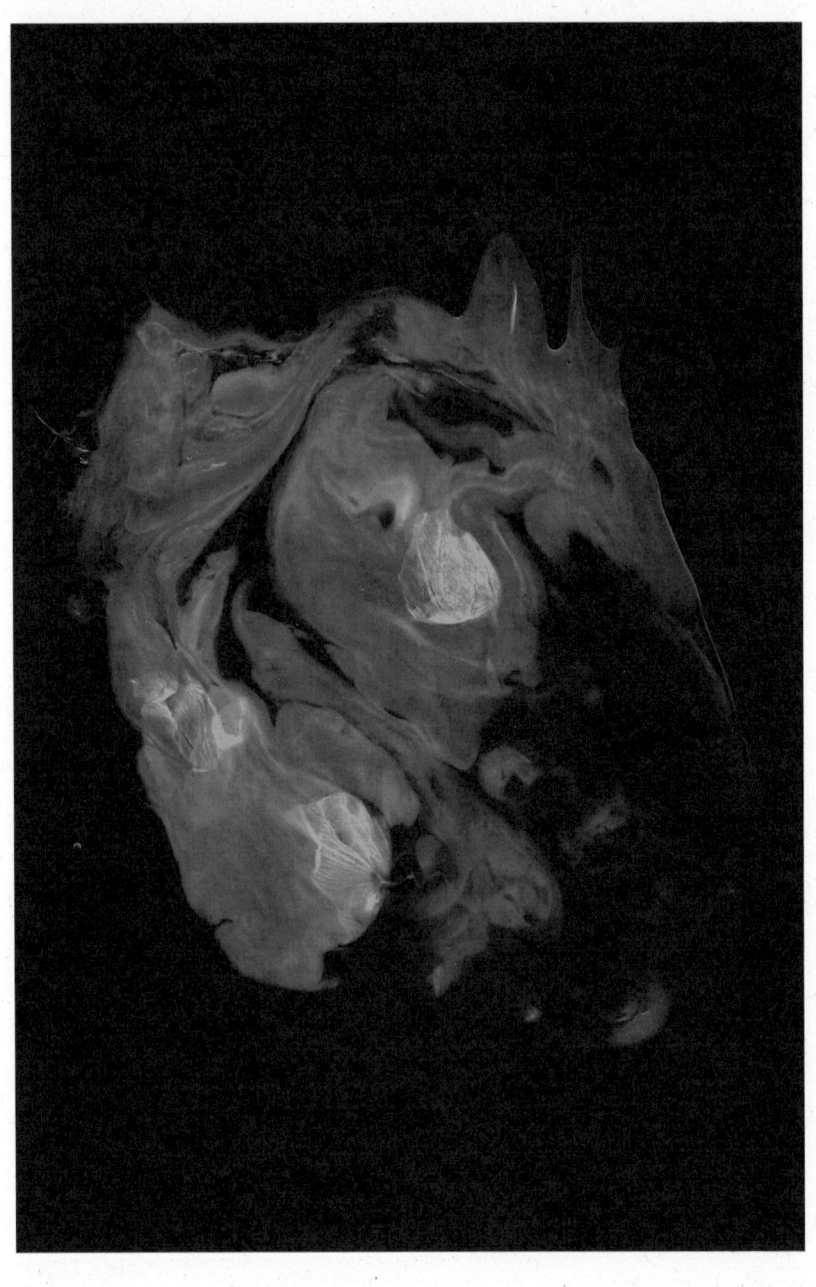

Ragnarök

Fizz of gossip along the vennels of the Earth. Old linking veins where sea nudges shoulders with the loch and whispers: What now? They expect the eels reply. Those secretive snakes. Everyone knows their long mercurial bodies are lined with stories. Yet now they only shake their heads and shiver their dorsal webbing like coquettish fans. "Listen, we'll tell you," we whisper, but we are still too small to send a tremor through the sea.

"The World Health Organisation declares Artemia Kyesia a Public Health Emergency of International Concern."

It will be a weird age, a wind age, a belching, bloody ice age. Hear that now? C-rack. It begins like this, with a crack! With a crack! We chatter to each other, telling it over and over excitedly, competing to say 'crack' the loudest, to make our siblings jump. CRACK! The littlest of us leaps into the air and we all fall about laughing.

One night, a huge iceberg launches itself into the ocean. CRACK! (One of the biggest shouts again into the ether, but now that we have laughed, greatly, once, the joke is done. We dig him in the ribs with our tails to shush him. We all know who tells it best.) The waves lick the iceberg all over, dribbling. In the morning, the bay is white with phlegm and scurf and the iceberg in the middle, dipping and bobbing, is smooth and glossy as a lozenge. Stretching for miles above it, on the exposed new face of the glacier, there is a thin fracture like a long black hair.

Over a number of days, curious fingers of saltwater poke into the gap and slowly winch it open. The ice sighs. The sun, rising over the white sea, dilates it further. Algae begins to bloom. It takes weeks, but finally the heat reaches us. We stir. We remember this. Neck cricked helixes uncurling ourselves, stiff with years of wait. The mineral smell of meltwater. Each one of us, a tiny twist of white bones, big eyed as brine shrimp.

That night, we catch a ride on the great, jellyfishing bubbles that rise through the endless tar black water. Nothing to see here. Then cresting, bursting, ears popping, we scatter. We scintillate. Buoyed upon the effulgent foam, the new sun extends her whiskers and we, warm for the first time in millennia, giggle as she tickles our toes. This was our start.

"Mode of transmission remains unknown. The Committee has issued advice on protecting yourself from infection with thorough hand-washing, washing clothes, towels and bed linen at a high heat, and avoiding consumption of raw fish."

We came to settle here. Reservoired in the clastic earth, we mud sludge kelpies are squidged into the nooks and nestles of the pebbles. The eels come slithering over the sand, back into the loch. We hear them, calling to the scaled, fanged and backward beasts that lurk here; "Do you still seek to know?" We gaze up at their white bellies and we sing; "We know, we know." Everyone ignores us.

Then the pump gates creak. A shudder through the bed. The other animals take hold of weeds and dig themselves into the sand. On the water, we are lifted. Gushing with glee, we bounce and tumble over each other, down into the streaming river.

We splish splash whee along the tributaries, diving headfirst down chutes, paddling through sewers. We watch our brothers and sisters get crushed in locks, big spinning corkscrews, mashing their heads against the rock over and over again. We wince. We get good at wiggling through sieves. We get a taste for chlorine, fluoride. It makes our heads spin and our eyes bulge but we don't mind it. We like limescale. The way it clings to our thin skin makes us feel armoured like adults. Our bellies rumble with excitement. Around us, big pink mouths shut.

"The parasite causes the sudden onset of symptoms such as; bloating; abdominal pain; fatigue; increased appetite; and nausea."

We sing for each other still from our separate, purple parrocks. Our bodies are changing, strangely, filling out. Our bones thicken and protrude. Our skin stretches and grows hard. Our tails extend and acquire a strong hinge which helps us snatch for food. To ease the hunger pains that plague us. Our bellies growl. Our new bones ache. We gobble down detritus that churns past us, or dig and snuffle for morsels in our spongy nests. Soon we are the size of anchovies, then sardines, one day we will be mackerel swimming in our sticky caves. We are afraid. We press our ears against the walls and listen desperately for that endless echo of 'me too'. At least, I do.

"Please do not go to hospital, unless you experience very severe abdominal cramping for more than four hours, or significant blood loss."

I have told the story a thousand times, just as our mother told me when she left us there, bathing in the lake, before the frost crept in. The end was always: the big pink mouth shuts. I have never deviated.

"The Committee has assembled an independent council of lawyers and scientists to determine the legal status of embryonic Artemia Kyesia, ahead of the parliamentary debate regarding the use of banned Misoprostol pills to accelerate the expulsion of larvae that have implanted in the womb."

I feel certain I am still alive though nothing remains that I recognise. I strain my ears for my siblings' singing, but still I hear only the gurgle of her gut, the rasp of her breath, the squelch of her sweat, the valves of her heart opening and the blood flooding out. When I first arrived, I wandered round the warren of her body for a while before I settled here, in her warm, most mud-like snug. I lick the walls. A little metallic but not unpleasant. I sleep a while. I wake and stretch and find that an inch has been added to my flicking, silver tail. I sing for my siblings. I curl into as small a ball as I can manage, tucking the tail back into my centre. I have always been small and able to hide. Now I must dodge the crushing of my cave as she spasms and squeezes against me. Now I must dig my bony spines into her as she sluices her insides out. I wonder how much longer I can hang in here. I wish for the eels to tell me what they see.

"Two women have died from complications relating to haemorrhage of the cervix when attempting to deliver full term Kyesia. The calves are stable. One woman is known to have died from rupture of the Fallopian tube prior to delivery. In this case, the calf also died."

One of my fins has been caught behind my back for an eternity and I cannot retrieve it. The soft part of my neck is pressed against a tranche of hard material, likely a bone, and I worry that if I grow any larger, my head will be bent further and my spine will snap. I have stopped eating but I think perhaps when I am sleeping, my mouth has rolled open and morsels have slipped in. My fin is going dead. I would not mind if it fell off. This is hell. I am certain. I am always hungry. It is unbearably hot. I may die here unless I can gnash a hole in the wall.

"The "Seahorse Bill" on the legal Status and Rights of Artemia Kyesia, includes rigorous protections against the dangerous removal of gestating Kyesia. The first trials under the new law begin tomorrow."

Hot, dry hands wrench me out. I pull back, whinnying, from the searching light. They drop me, moaning, into the loch. The water splits around my face. I fall endless, spinning, through the blue which is shot with glinting bubbles. I remember the beginning. I was much, much smaller then and could not sink. As the light and warmth seeps into inky black, I scrabble away from that. I find new use for these feathered appendages. They carve the water apart and I heft myself determinedly into the gap, climbing towards the warbling light, back the way I came. As I rise into a greener strata of the water where pondweed and insects float, the oxygen seeps more easily through my gills. I break the surface, with a radiant hiccup, and look up at her. Her face is not as I imagined. Nothing like my mother. The creature on the bank has no hard edges. She is round and fluffy and glistening with moisture. Her eyes meet mine. They are shot red as her inside, a trickle of which is now melding with the lake. Fine threads of tissue tangled around my spines. Her long limbs are wrapped around another of her kind. They swell against each other and I hear them sing a long low note that makes my fronds twinge and prickle. I sing back to them. My voice sounds hoarse. I have not used it in so long. She points at me then, so sharply that I imagine that tremulous finger pushing my jaws open, sliding down my throat, the nail catching jaggedly on my tonsils, down down to my own wet cave. Strange and thrilling, she bares her teeth and her mouth opens and a sound comes weeping out of her. "Mornstar." I say it to myself.

"We are distressed by the reports of hostility and violence outside of the Court today. In the capital, the threat level has been raised to critical."

She seems shocked by the sound she has emitted. She chokes and buries her face deeper in the other creature's breast. She lets out a desperate moan. She clutches her abdomen, where we were knotted to one another. This reminds me where I've been. I turn to face the endless, dark and churning water, her blood indistinguishable from it now. I sink under the lake, which is colder than she ever was. I swim silently away. An echo bumps about inside my brain. "Mornstar," it sings, "Mornstar."

"Several arrests were made this morning. Reportedly, the charges include harassment, heresy, riot and a range of terrorism offences, including dissemination of terrorist publications."

I am afraid.

"Approximately five million calves were delivered by the specially trained midwives last week."

A glint of gold as her fin slices the water, a skitter of insects on the surface, a shadow passing under the lily pads. I dip my head under the water and hum. A long, warm note of recognition. Above me the water shatters, a million sparkling droplets shaken over my back. She leaps onto me, flipping me over onto my belly. We grip each other, and roll and roll in the lake, tangling ourselves in the lily pads and tossing them into the air like old salad. All afternoon, we sing and swim and kiss. The next day, more of us arrive and we greet them like we would welcome the regrowth of an injured limb.

"Early observation of Kyesic young that have detached from their host body indicate impressive juvenile growth rates, comparable to that of blue whales."

We continue to grow every day. We fatten til our shadows blot the moon's rippling reflection. We shout across the valleys: "Look at this!" Then leap and twirl into the sky, shaking our spiny fins like manes. Water spins out from us and rains upon the meadows. We belly flop back into the water, sending waves across the valley. It gushes through the high street of the village; the cats leap onto the walls.

"We anticipate further flooding in low-lying areas of the country in the coming days."

The littlest of us clap their fins together in the feeder rivers, and wobble their keels in delight. The water crashes up around them, showering them with droplets. They lick their snouts and nibble the grass and weeds that flank them.

"Recent flash flooding has been attributed to natural fluctuations in sea levels and increased rainfall in the early summer season from the polar ice thawing."

Each day, as they grow, their sides are squeezed tighter against the banks. They slap their tails onto the verge to let the dammed water flow, then roll themselves heavily back into their cradles. Soon they will have to move on, riding the torrents to deeper waters.

"The new compensation scheme will help support farmers and landowners. All farmers that are able to prove that their land has never previously been at risk of flooding will be eligible."

We look round and nod that we all like this loch. The sweep of trees that line each side, the sandy bottom to scrape our itchy backs against, the sheep that sometimes float across for us to snaffle up, the familiar hiss and crackle of the eel plant at the tail end. We watch the people use big nets to scoop the eels out of the water. They squirm like gorgon heads. We taunt them for not knowing their own fate. It makes us feel better about ourselves.

"Incidence of postpartum psychosis, including aural hallucinations, amongst those that delivered Kyesic calves stands at twenty in every thousand."

We rarely talk about our time apart. It was a dark, maroonish time. When we think about it, it is like tracing a bruise, skirting the edge of an old pain. But though we enjoy this loch during the day, and all the games we play (nosing in the mud for grubs, skimming stones with our tongues, combing our fronds with teasels), in the night many of us sleep with one eye open against the distant singing of our creatures, which sometimes slips out of our mouths. Mornstar? We are woken by this uneasy lullaby, and begin to sing it too, as we do when we do not understand. We find it helps to taste the sound on our own tongues to uncover a song's meaning.

I recognise my creature's song on the voices of my siblings. I nudge my closest sister and tell her the song's origin. She nods and whispers back to me "I see, I see. My creature held me and sang 'Maybe Nora.'" We both sang Maybe Nora Mornstar and decided they might mean the same thing. Our littler sister, feeling left out, said "Mine said Ariel?" Then our siblings all began to chime in with their own lonely song that had been going round in their heads. A flurry of strange discordant sounds. "Damon?" "Marina?" "Mary like my mother?" Another of us went quite starry eyed and said "Mine stroked my ears and said leetulwon over and over and I still hear her now singing it." It is hard to get our tongues around all the different words. Our biggest brother hears our whispering and says, with weathered wisdom: "It is a name. We each have our own." Our own. None of us had never owned a thing and now we each have two – a creature and a name. "It is how they tell you from me." Me, Mornstar. He looks at me, over the great expanse of our siblings' bodies and says: "Don't worry, we will forget them soon."

"Local hubs providing sandbags, medical supplies, food, dry clothing and transport have been established around the country."

It is nighttime and our games are over. We are clustered in the bowl of the loch, nestling down to sleep. It is a squeeze now. Someone pipes up from the edge, saying that someone else keeps kicking them in the back. Someone else, closer to the middle, pleads that their fin is going dead. Someone groans that there isn't any room. We all purse our lips and try not to breathe. Someone in the centre, a tiny quivering voice, begins to sing: "Let's go to the sea." One by one we join the throng. The sound rises over the water, over the valley, like a mist and from every loch and pond and river the same song comes.

"Huge numbers of Kyesia spotted 'playing' in the English Channel."

The largest and most impatient of us have already tobogganed across the grass, snagging our great bellies on trees and using our muscular tails to steer us. They leave in the morning, chasing the fleeing eels. From their singing, we learn that it is not far to the ocean, and that there is space there to stretch. We apologise to the people as we pass, the tumult of our wafting fronds sucking boats under the foam.

"Sea levels: redacted. Death toll: redacted."

We cannot stop it now, except by bashing our heads against the cliffs until we sink and rot. (Our bones rise like gulls to split the sky). There are so many of us and we are so large, that if we lie nose to tail, we encircle the earth completely. We bite each other to form a ring and our blood turns the ocean pink. The sand is stained with it in undulating lines. We live in the sea, in the lakes, straddling olympic swimming pools, in the rivers. In America, some of us live on land, where women climb up us each day to bathe us with hoses, and leave sprinklers near our foreheads. They call us babies, though we are larger than their yards. We are still growing. We feel the itch of new cells as we sing. The sea is rising to meet us, to keep us warm and safe and together. We watch it swallow the towns we were born in. We have watched them from afar. Each of us flinches alone when our own weeping creature drowns.

"This government declares that there are no unknown animals. All references to sightings of uncategorised megafauna are hereby banned from circulation by both organisations and individuals. Alleged evidence of such sightings is hereby banned from circulation by both organisations and individuals. Written and spoken use of the terms "Water horse", "Leviathon", "Midgard", "Each-Uisge", "Kelpie", "Aughisky", "Monster", "Serpent" are hereby banned."

There is only water now. We can no longer swim beside each other. The uniform pulsing of our tails whips up towering waves that come round the earth the other way to dunk our heads and slap our eyes. So we drift apart. Over our shoulders, we sing back: What are you called? The wind has picked up and our voices are tossed on its currents. No names come back to us through the howling gale. We swim around above the empty cities, now sea and loch have merged. We sing: Where are you? But we only catch shadows of each other. The littlest of us hide from the largest, who are hungry once again. We sing: What now?

The eels whisper in their small voices: Do you still seek to know? We do not hear them. The sky is black. We roar, and as we do, there is a bright white light and an almighty crack.

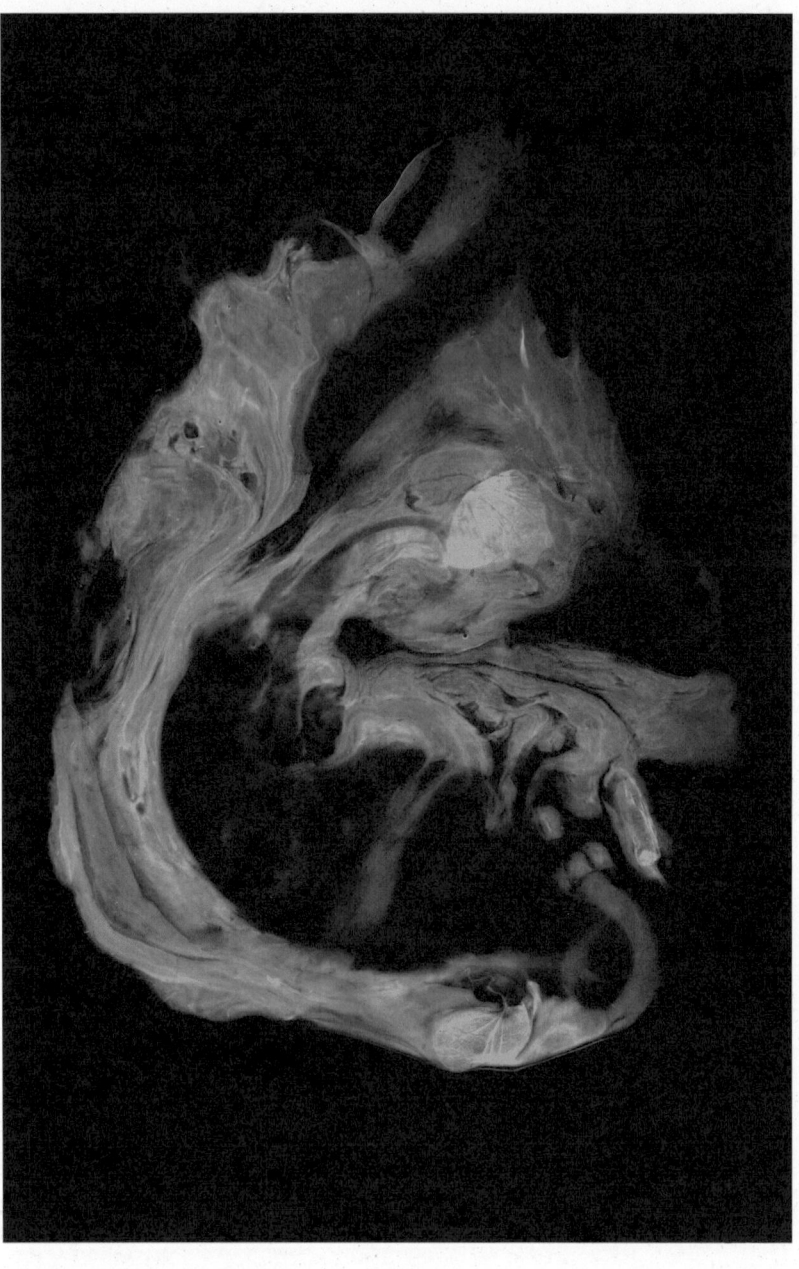

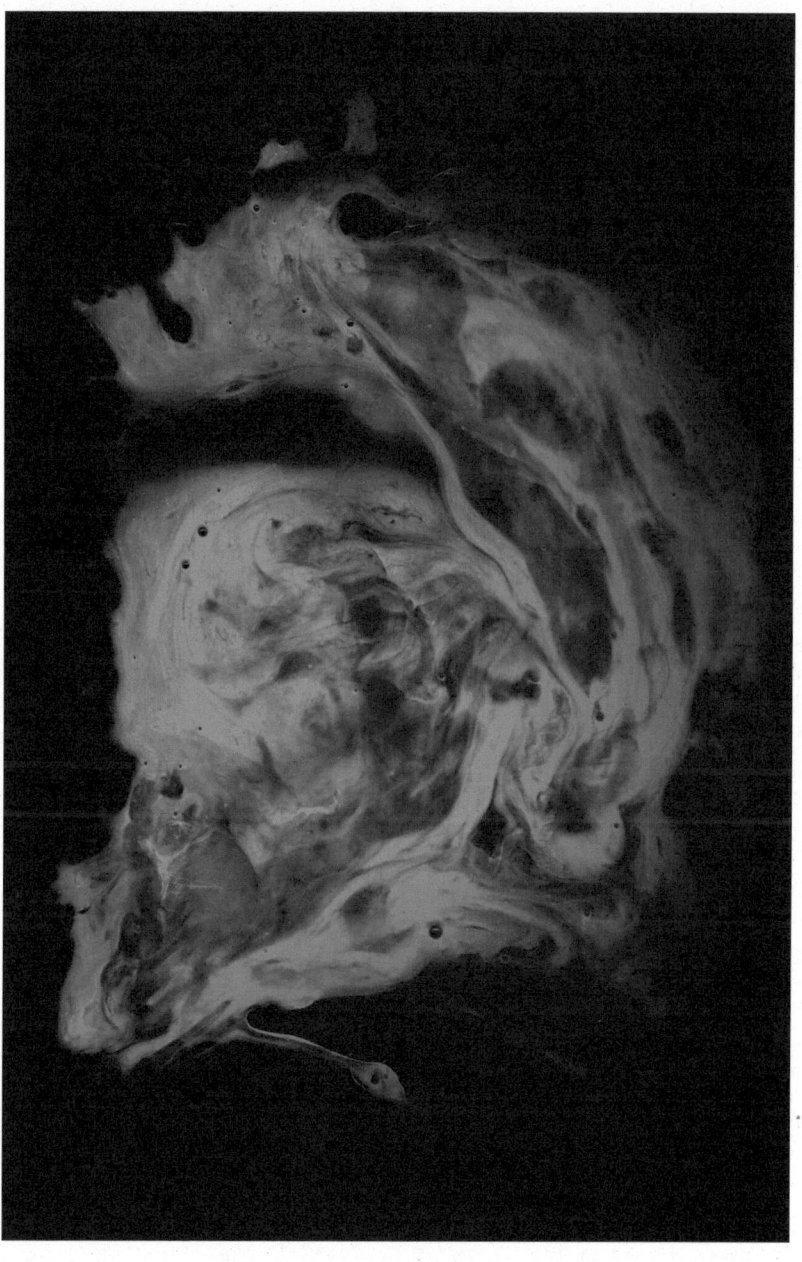

A Childhood
Experience of Yellow

The summer that I turn seven, we go to stay with my uncle and his wife on their farm for a whole two weeks. Each morning, I am thrust into the mastery of my big cousin, Ella. She crosses her arms and says she does not see why she has to look after the baby. She rolls her eyes, throws her chin back and huffs like a horse shaking a fly from its nostril. I fear she will pull my arm out of its socket as she yanks me behind her into the garden. She likes four games; calling me baby while she combs my hair; hide and seek, in which she is always losing interest and wandering off; a game called dares (in dares, she makes me do things like put my hand inside holes in trees and steal change from coat pockets); and Ella's favourite game is not what I call a game because it does not have rules and you cannot call time out. In this game she just tells me things to try and scare me. Once she told me that in the barn they cut the heads off chickens and the dead chickens run around for the rest of the day, spurting blood from their severed necks. Sometimes they escape from the barn and run into the house. I said I didn't believe her and to prove it, she shoved me into the barn to look at the axe and the blood stain on the wooden stump. I wet myself. It soaked through my jeans, squelching in my sandals and mushing in the sawdust. Since then, Ella tries to spook me most days. Today she points out every creepy crawly in the garden in a witchy voice. The beetles and bugs that pour out of the flowers, the great yellow slugs on the back of the shed, and the monstrous centipedes under the flowerpots. She lifts up a log and drips woodlice on my upturned palm. I stick my nose in the air and declare that I am not scared. I think to myself, proudly, that I quite like insects. Their antennae and little legs waving in the air. The inkblot patterns on their backs. They all scuttle and shrink from Ella's big feet, crunching through the grass, but when she slopes off, sick of me, and leaves me squatting quietly in the dirt, they venture out again. A clutch of beetles appear on a leaf, glinting brilliant green, their armoured backs splitting into fine wings. Now I am alone in the garden, I become Queen of the Insects, and these are my guards.

As Queen of the Insects, I have certain powers. I command the spiders to sneak into Ella's wellingtons and scuttle up her legs. Satisfied, I nod farewell to the beetles and remove my crown. I can hear the distant murmurings of adults and the squawking of the hens. This part of the garden is hidden from the cottage. My arms and legs tingle with the thrill of being alone. I shuffle my bum more squarely on the ground, and cross my legs. I close my eyes. I much prefer pretending to playing games, especially Ella's. I pretend I have red ringlets and live on the farm. Except it's the farm as it was a hundred years ago, so Ella isn't there and I am wearing a dress and a white apron. I stand up and address a toddler at my knee. I pull some leaves off the brambles and stuff them into my pockets. Money is always tight but we sell strawberries and eggs to get by. I make some piles from the leaves and count them worriedly. I make shooing sounds and a sour face like my mother. I stand up and put my hands on my hips. I have several goats. I have to sweep them out of the kitchen, telling them off for eating the slippers. On my farm, we do not decapitate the animals, not even the chickens.

My father finds me in a reverie, stirring my leaves with a stick, mud on my knees and streaking my arms. He crouches next to me. "Where has Ella gone?" I shrug. He is silent for a moment. He holds a finger up to the leaf and one of the beetles walks onto his nail, "It's a Rose Chafer. Isn't that a pretty name?" I look up at him. He whispers conspiratorially into my ear, "Come with me. I've got something to show you."

I skip next to him, swinging on his arm, my hand warm inside his. We sit down beside each other, by the chicken coop, and I lean gently into his musky, aniseed smell. The coop looks exactly like the cottage but in miniature. It would be the perfect size for dolls. My father opens up the roof and I stand on my tiptoes to see inside. There, nestled in the straw, are a huddle of little chicks. Their yellow wool is streaked with grey and clods of dirt. My father says, "You can have one if you would like." They turn their heads quizzically up at us. They have black glossy eyes like the beads in my mother's jewellery box, which she lets me sift through when I am poorly.

My father pours a chick into my cupped hands and tells me to take it into the house. I can keep it forever. "We'll put it in a box and you can take it home," he says. I ask him where it will live. "Can it live in my room?" I ask hopefully. He shakes his head, grinning. He tells me that we can build a hen house of our own. He tells me to hold it very tightly so it doesn't hop away. It is so soft. It is the softest thing I have ever held. I can feel its feet scratching at my palms and the restless throbbing of its tiny heart. With my finger I stroke the ripple of its ribs. A little cage moving rapidly. Its bones must be like pins. I worry it might trickle through my fingers like sand. I startle at the jerking of its head as it tries to peck my fingers apart. My father laughs at my bulging eyes. "Hold it tight now."

All the way up the garden path I focus fiercely on holding it still and tight. It is so warm snuggled into the nest of my fingers. I worry my father will tell me off if I drop it or let it run away. He might even make me carry it back to the coop. I try to pretend I am a farmer, who is always hiding a chick in her apron pocket. Instead of this, I imagine the chick falling out of my hands, where it would surely be ripped to shreds by one of Ella's cats, or a dog, or a fox. The cats swing their tails from low branches as we pass. I can feel that the chick is scared. Its whole body seems to thrum with nervous life. My father strides ahead of me. I am filled with so strong a love that I can hardly breathe. I hold my chick close to me, right up to my chest where I imagine it can feel my heart beating as stridently and fearfully as its own.

When we come into the kitchen, my father opens a special tin with holes stabbed into the lid and holds it out to me. He says I can put the chick in there. Ella comes over to look. I shake my head at my dad. I do not want to open my hands. I bite my lip. The chick is still. My tummy rolls. Ella tugs at my fingers. I do not want to open my hands. She dares me. The chick's limp body tumbles into the box, like an old hanky. It looks odd, flat. Its wiry legs that had so furiously scratched at me lie at an awkward angle. My lip quivers. My father puts the lid on the tin and says nothing. I burst into tears.

I was so afraid then, of the silence all around me; the yellow silence of the chick, radiating from the tin; of Ella's silence, her hand still clamped upon my wrist; of my father's hesitation before he gathered me into his arms, hush-hushing my sobs and holding me tight against his chest. Finally, my ear pressed to his heart, so I could hear it beating, real and steady and loud like a fist.

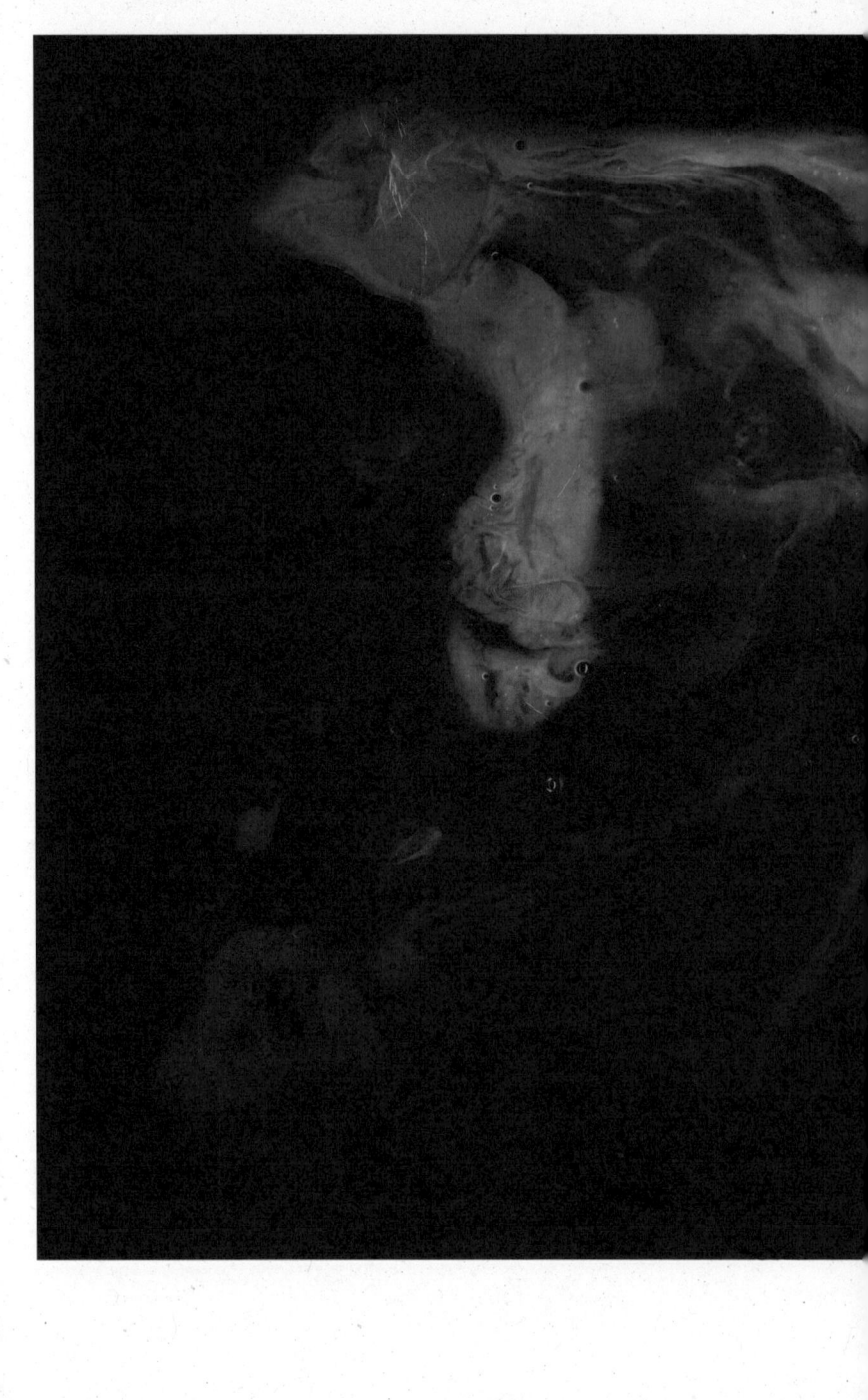

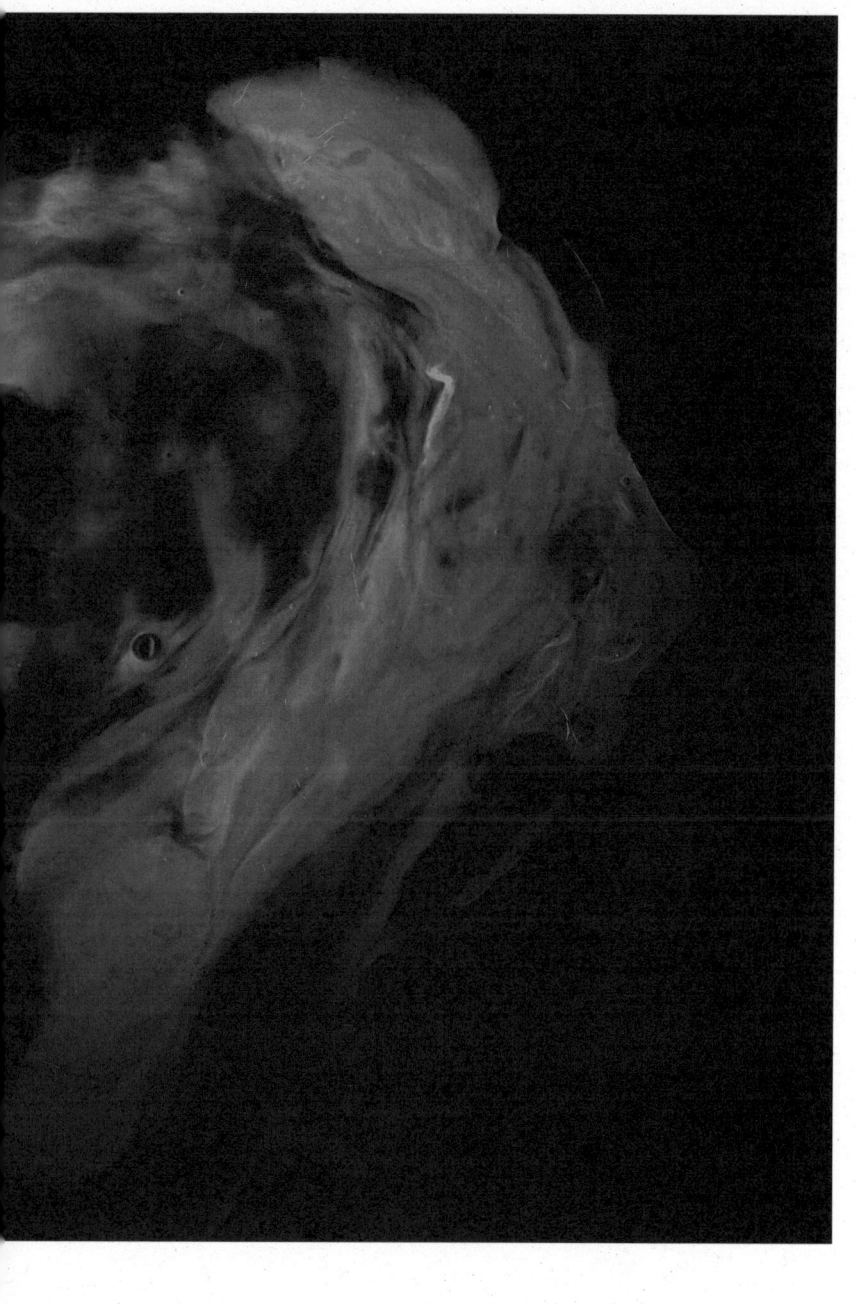

Keeping Sheila

The queue in the pet shop shambled forward. It was a Thursday afternoon, just after three. All these people should be working, Alice thought. She had an appointment at half past four in Stratford. It would take at least an hour to wiggle her way across London. The tupperware wobbled in Alice's hands. The Terror was butting its ugly head against the lid, threatening to pop it off and leap into her face. Alice flicked it through the lid.

Alice wondered if she should let Patrick know what she was doing. Since he'd packed his stuff, Alice had been lumbered with a looming sense that Patrick would ask for the axolotls back, or insist that they shared custody, shuttling the tank between their flats in overpriced Ubers. She imagined him hoiking the tank under one arm and cycling off wobbly down the road, the axolotls slapping around, aswirl with pebbles and soggy fish flakes.

The shop was a relic of an extinct high street shopping culture. The door was propped open with a grotesque plaster figurine of a dalmatian with a lolling tongue. The window featured a sun-bleached selection of leaflets for dog walkers, groomers, cat rescues, and the obligatory poster for Zippo's Circus. Stacked cages and tanks flanked either side of the galley leading up to the counter. The wall above the counter displayed a perverse selection of leads, collars and squeaky toys.

Alice was stood behind a man, about her age, in the queue. She surveyed him, quietly. He was wearing jeans and a crisply ironed shirt. She regarded the unchewed hems of this immaculate ensemble and concluded that he did not own a pet. At most, he was a houseplant person. Cacti, Alice speculated, in their arid soil, blossoming from his neglect. She imagined he would be an uncomplicated, but effective, lover. She had always liked imagining how sex with strangers would feel. Alice wondered what the other customers might think about her. She was obviously neither a cat nor a dog person. She hoped she did not look like a keeper of mice. She hoped she looked like she'd be adequate in bed, though that didn't matter so much for women. The man turned his head, as if he sensed her thinking about him.

Alice dropped her eyes. The Terror was floating on its back now, provocatively displaying its pale belly to her. Patrick came vaguely to mind with his white belly streaked with black hair and the smattering of pink, scaly regions of impetigo. Stretched over her bed, feet flopping, he'd gaze into the tank while Alice yanked her knickers up and thrashed around in an inside-out jumper. Patrick would place a finger on the glass and Bradley - the christian name for The Terror - would glide, oozingly, up from the bed of the tank to lay a webbed paw against the glass, perhaps offering a few sucking kisses. Patrick would grin, "Alice, look! He's high-fiving me."

She shuddered. Bradley rose slowly from the water. His grey pearl eyes regarded Alice suspiciously. The pink fronds that crowned his face fanned and his webbed hands stirred the water villainously.

Alice swapped the tupperwares. The second tupperware contained the other, victimised axolotl; Sheila. Sheila was a runty albino alien with blue speckling round her eyes like an insomniac, and a fine, feathery beard of green slime. She swam round and round in circles conjuring a gurgling whirlpool. She always swam clockwise nowadays, her surviving right arm scooping determinedly.

Alice looked beyond the caged rodents to the serenely swimming fish at the front of the shop. She pressed her thumbs a little harder into the side of Sheila's container as if she could impart her thoughts to the axolotl this way. Soon Sheila would be cosied up in one of those palatial tanks with the colourful pebbles and plastic seagrass.

Sheila was depressed. Alice knew that she had not been happy for a long time, but when Alice brought it up, Patrick dismissed her concerns as the kind of anthropomorphic psychobabble that lined vets' pockets. Even before the assault, Sheila had spent all day lying on her side in the corner of the tank, unmoved by Patrick's cooing. He'd sometimes give her a flick, or rap his fingers on the glass, and she'd roll over to not look at him. After a month or so, Matthew had grouchily announced that Sheila could be "Alice's one". Alice did not point out that technically both of them were hers.

The man stepped up to the counter. With a deep public school drawl, he ordered five frozen mice. As he squeezed past her, out of the shop, the cold blue carrier bag brushed Alice's calf. Alice was horrified that she had contemplated having sex with him.

The shop assistant beckoned her forwards. "Madam?" With one word, he had aged her. Alice placed the tupperware boxes on the counter.

"I want to return these," she announced firmly.

"These little guys?" Just the kind of insipid americanism Alice expected from a pet person. He opened the tupperwares, one by one. "What are they?" Alice looked around the shop desperately. Surely, she was not the resident amphibian expert.

"Axolotls."

"So, we only accept returns of live animals in exceptional circumstances." Alice tried to explain the exceptional circumstance she had found herself in. A guinea-pig meeped.

"I am sorry to hear that, madam. That must have been very distressing."

Alice actually hadn't been as distressed by the axolotl's cannibalism as the shop assistant implied. She had excellent presence of mind. She had rolled up her sleeves and plunged her arms into the tank. She had deftly unlatched Bradley's jaw with her finger and gently eased the frayed remains of Sheila's arm out of his mouth. Then she had scooped Sheila out of the tank, and carried her to the bathroom. Twice, Sheila had almost slipped out of her hand like a bar of soap in the shower, but Alice held her firmly. Sheila soared through space, one arm desperately pawing at the air, her gills opening and closing rapidly. Sheila's persistence in the face of such devastation was admirable. Alice mused that it was a quality that they shared, as she measured the bathwater's temperature with a sugar thermometer.

This distinguishing quality of pragmatism had resulted in numerous accusations of coldness and emotional unavailability. Once, Patrick had declared that she was "icy and impenetrable." Alice had shrugged it off. He had flapped his hands in the air, crying to an absent jury, "See!" Patrick was often personally offended that Alice did not take his slights to heart.

There was a ruminating silence while the shop assistant looked glumly at Sheila.

"You know, this kind of aggressive behaviour is quite common, particularly if pets are not separated, or are underfed." Alice felt an acid blurt of indignation, but she swallowed it down. She had dutifully dished out their fish flakes every morning, often before she made herself tea. She explained that she still wanted to return them.

"Do you have a receipt?" Alice produced a birthday card from a torn silver envelope. Folded inside it was a perfectly crisp gift receipt. "Ok, I'm just going to take a closer look at them," Alice pushed the boxes across the counter. She checked the time on her phone. She had fifty-seven minutes. She began to map and recalculate routes in her head. The shop assistant looked up at Alice expectantly and cleared his throat, "Madam?"

"Sorry, what's the verdict?" She was becoming her father.

"I'm happy to offer you an exchange or full refund for the

green axolotl. The white axolotl is not in a resaleable condition so we can only accept her in exchange for partial credit."

"But axolotls grow back their limbs." This much Alice knew. When Patrick had presented them to her, he had given her an extended lecture on their many charming attributes. The more Patrick explained why she would love them, the more offended Alice was by the gift. But then she looked at how Patrick was crouched in front of the tank, grinning, and realised that Patrick had bought them for himself.

"That's true," the shop assistant conceded reluctantly.

"So there's nothing wrong with her?" She immediately regretted snapping. Presence of mind, Alice. The shop assistant narrowed his eyes and restated the shop's policy. From her tub Sheila looked up at him, and then back at Alice.

"Cash or credit?"

—

Alice was five minutes late to her appointment, but the receptionist beamed and kindly admonished the traffic in London. She was directed to a sofa and a fan of gossip magazines to choose from. There was a lovely soapy smell in the clinic.

If Patrick found out, he would be furious that she had not simply put a glass divider in the tank. He had always spoken about that idea with the rue fondness that a retired guard might speak about Guantanamo. Alice could see it; Bradley viciously smashing his head against the glass and Sheila cowering in a far corner, the tiny flower of a new hand budding from her armpit.

Alice selected a gossip rag and flipped through to the personal experience section, which always made her feel better about herself. Alice hadn't been surprised when Patrick broached the subject of moving in with Rosie, but she had been offended by how condescending he was when he delivered the news. Patrick had rubbed her back and explained in a slow and caring voice that it wasn't that he didn't love her, it was just that they wanted different things. Alice assumed a parallel conversation was happening between Rosie and her very tall boyfriend Max. Patrick apologised earnestly for keeping his feelings for Rosie a secret. Alice admitted that she had known for some time. "What?" He lifted his hand from her back and stood up, unable to process this deviation from the script. As Patrick raged on about her martyrdom, Alice thought about Max. When she had seen him at the office Christmas party, the length of his legs had not escaped her notice. As Patrick wheeled his bike through the gate in a fury, she called after him, "I'm keeping the axolotls," and slammed the door. She listened to him wrestle with his panniers and smiled smugly. Alice had always been better at keeping secrets.

A doctor in a baby blue tunic summoned Alice into a little room. The doctor had a neat, scrubbed face, her hair scraped back into a tight bun. Alice hopped onto the bed and slid her knickers off.

A week ago Alice had gone to see her sister, Evie, to fill her in on the unfolding domestic drama. Alice's niece, who was young and wily enough to still be precocious rather than rude, had greeted Alice at the door and said, cheerily, that she looked pregnant. Evie had exclaimed in a teetering voice, "Of course she's not pregnant!" and swept the little girl into her arms, tutting. She had turned to Alice, ushering her in, and said: "I think you are looking very slim."

Alice had taken a pregnancy test that evening. She had stared at the pink cross blithely. She made a list of pros; she knew the cons by rote. She phoned the abortion clinic that afternoon and made an appointment for half past four the following Tuesday.

Patrick had lauded the fact that Alice was not a maternal person, just as she was not a pet person, as one of her most attractive traits. He brought it up a lot, mostly when they walked past clods of mothers walking their dogs and offspring in the park. Patrick had even brought it up when he unveiled the axolotls, explaining how they reminded him of her. "They eat their own eggs," he'd said, like she would understand.

But it wasn't that Alice didn't want kids, more that she didn't mind not having them. Which was how she felt about pets too, mostly. She had briefly convinced herself that she was barren, and accepted this fact when Patrick went through a phase of ejaculating inside her and still no foetus had presented itself. He had accepted her deficiency, never once thinking it could be him.

Lying on the bed in the clinic, Alice's resolve crystallised. Patrick did not need to know. She closed her eyes and smiled, imagining him bumping into her in the supermarket, her swollen belly blooming beneath a jumper. As Alice dreamed, Sheila bobbed pleasantly in her tupperware and smiled beadily up at the ultrasound screen.

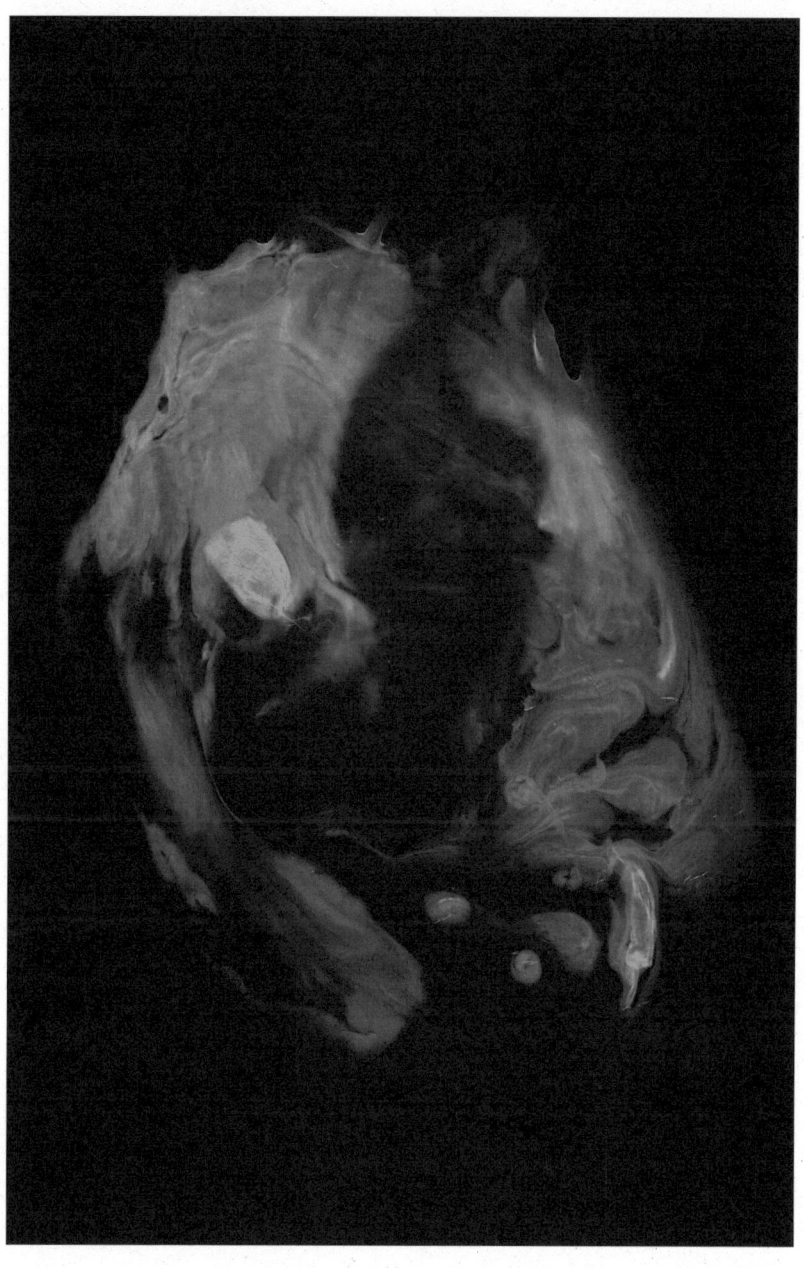

Like Diamonds

The wooden platform juts over the lip of the lake, skimming over the water like a raft. At one end a ladder drops into the lake. Spider webs stretch across its rungs, heavy with beads of water that glitter like diamonds in the failing sun. The water is thick and brown with silt that hennas the tiny hairs on the girls' bodies. The apricot of the sky is held, preserved on the water's surface for a moment, a breath, before it is marbled by their arms and legs kicking as they chase each other round and round. It has been a hot day, the sun grilling their shoulders and singeing the tender leaves of young trees. The lake, which is more of a pond, has been warming up all day so that the first thirty centimetres are bath warm. By their second lap, this sun soaked strata has been whisked into the inkier depths and their skin prickles with cold. Their burnt shoulders sigh in giddy delight.

They climb out, shivering. The first girl winches herself up rung by rung, her white legs red as radishes. The second girl treads water, her left foot stirring some algae around. She looks up at the first girl's ascending body. Trains her eyes on the spot where the polyester fabric gathers in folds, on the ties that snake around her hips and swing, dripping, against her thighs. The silvery sheen of suncream applied too late on the base of her spine, that place where her own thumbs had been. She scoops the water round her. The water boatmen skitter out of her grasp. A little whimper of pleasure, for her sunburn looks lilac in this light. Water droplets from her hair travel in rills down her back and quiver like icicles on the untucked label of her bikini bottoms until, finally overcome by their own weight, they snap and splash onto the upturned cheeks of the girl below. Quick then, it's freezing down here.

They lie beside each other, bellies on the grass, peering over the side of the lake. The water level is lower than it should be this time of year and the reeds are crisped and withering. An exodus of tiny frogs, no larger than a pinky fingernail, are crawling, leaping, freaking up the bank. Some are sand coloured, some like flakes of slate. So well camouflaged they'd be invisible if it wasn't for the thinking of their moist eyes and glistening backs. The girls jab their fingers at the frogs - that one, there, look. So strange that they began as black pupils in a breathing foam, their growth utterly exposed.

The girls turn onto their backs, their hips bumping. An itchy grass imprint crosshatching their bellies. One of them sits up and begins to pick the algae off her feet in long threads. She dangles it over her companion's face, teasing it on her lips which open in horror as it dips in. Cackling, spitting, hands snatching and slapping at her mouth. Gross. Gross. Gross. They hold each other in a furious stare that shatters into giggles. They lie back flat on the grass, hands on their heaving bellies, eyes turned to the abundant sky. They close their eyes until the sun burns blue scintillas into their retinas. They feel for one another's hands. Their feet seek the other's toes. Slowly, slowly, til her lips find the hot, coconutty nook behind her ear, the salty corner of her mouth, which moves to say I hate my thighs. Soon the thighs are kissed. Anything to please this little fisherwoman of tenderness.

A frog, the colour of pencil shavings, hops from the mud into the grass. As he navigates the forest of giant spears that slice his belly and tangle in his sticky hands, he finds himself crawling, slowly, slowly, through the sopping nest of their entangled hair. Algae, her, or dirt, it makes no difference to him, as he makes his steady pilgrimage. As long as there is shade and moisture, protection from the violent sun, everything is good.

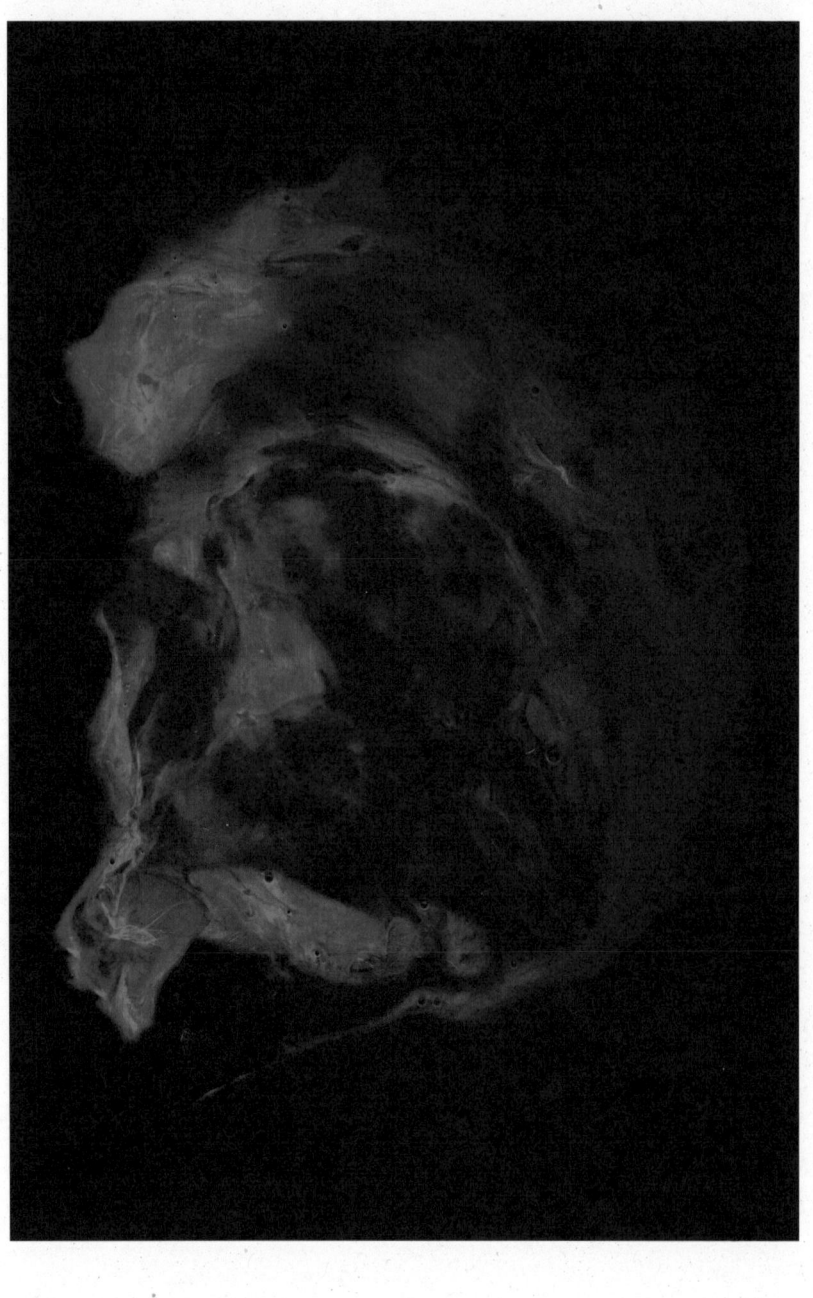

Real Life

On the first day there was a pair of shoes. Maple-coloured brogues with laces tugged and knotted so tight the sole curled up at the edges like a dried leaf. I picked the left one up and turned it over. The sole was worn down on the outside edge of the heel. The leather worn right away and the wood receding and exposed, ply after ply, in striations of pink and beige. Size 8. Small for a man. I recognised the name of the shoemaker, stamped into the sole and burnished away. Somewhere in West London there is a wooden form that has been used to hammer these shoes into the right shape. A selkie form with narrow toes and a high arch, with a number stencilled on in black. And in a leather-bound ledger in a back office, there is that same number - a dash - and then a name.

I put the shoe back down on the wall. I didn't know any men petite enough to squeeze into them. With everything else I had on, I didn't think about the shoes, the form, the laces or the name again all day. I was on my way to the lido, to swim. Up and down, driving my body through the water. The lido rinses my brain of all cognition except how fast my legs and arms are moving, whether my glutes are engaged, and the count. Five. Six. Twenty-four more to go. Each length is 50 metres. I do the sums in my head. What's that in miles, roughly? The shoes were washed clean away on the tide of imperial, calorie, velocity conversions, so that when I walked back up the hill, past the wall, I barely registered that they were gone.

The rest of the day was consumed by an endless monotony of errands that always precede my actually sitting at my desk to work. Laundry. Shopping. Stacking the dishwasher. Then I make coffee, brown toast, and I open my laptop. Here follows; an hour lost to flagging emails; a brief web.md journey from period cramps to gastroparesis; resending a photo to a man on hinge; following up with "Did you get this? My wifi is really shit."; review his facebook; quit all tabs. Then I open a blank document. My fingers trail on the keyboard. Dust has gathered in the grooves between the keys. There is a fine white hair above the space bar, a smattering of crumbs. I write blog posts. It covers my rent. I live alone in a one-bedroom flat. At the moment I write a lot about rental cars and skin care, but I have written pieces about vibrators, data security, the health benefits of CBD oil. Last month, a swimming costume company sent me a bikini and asked me to review it. I christened it the perfect combination of stretchy, sexy and supportive. They asked me to write a follow up piece.

The bikini is still in its plastic sleeve in the back of my knicker drawer, with the sanitary sticker attached. I put it on once, propped my phone on the windowsill and took nine pictures of my bum. I'd never wear a bikini to the lido. When I swim, I wear an ancient, wrinkling, green Speedo swimming costume with yellow racer stripes running over my hips like McDonald's arches. I have a routine. Every morning, I drag my sleep-thick body out of bed and pull tracksuit bottoms and a t-shirt over this trusty green suit. I shamble to the lido, swipe my card, leave my clothes in a pile on the side of the pool, drag my hair into a bun and tramp into the water. Cold water. When it hits my navel, I tip myself forward. My feet lift off the ground and I push against the tiled wall. I am swimming. There is a lethargy that can only be sluiced away like this. When I emerge from the pool, I am blotchy-thighed and pincer-eyed, vital and defiant. Cold water swimming, Wim Hof, all that, it's just will power, it's just endurance, it's like wrestling. This philosophy makes me an uncharitable swimmer, but a strong one; I overtake pregnant women and old ladies who are not using their back legs. It's worse to swim up someone's arse. It's all about momentum. Once your feet have left the wall, there is nothing to do but complete the length. And count. I make a note of the distance swum when I get out.

The day after the shoes there is a toy farm on the wall. It is packed into a Morrison's bag for life. I peep inside. My granny had a set like this. When I was little, I'd spend hours setting it all up on the floor, really tidy. You can sell these sets on eBay for decent money now. Behind the bag is an old copy of *Madeline*, the French picture book about an orphan being looked after by nuns. I loved that book. I contemplate taking the whole bag and the book, but I already have a towel and a water bottle, my debit card and my phone, and the walk to the lido is longer than you think. I rummage through the bag and extract three plastic horses. I put them in my pocket. I take a few steps, pause, and turn around. I pick up *Madeline* and tuck her under my armpit.

Walking back from the pool, wet-haired, I notice the bag is gone. I kick myself for not claiming it. Before I start writing my first blog post of the day, I look up the farm set on eBay and curse myself again. I arrange the three horses on my desk as if they are braying for a race. I am thankful, at least, that my competitor did not get the full set.

After this near miss, I check the wall each day on my way to the lido. Always, there are fresh treasures. A cut glass ashtray, a brown leather belt, an unopened box of cotton handkerchiefs, a thin volume with a titillating title called *A Safer Place to Cry* by Dr Brian Roet. I start to carry my things in a copious ecru tote bag so I can claim bigger objects; hardbacks; framed pictures; a salad bowl. About a week after the arrival of the shoes, the gate is open when I pass by and a skip has been established in the driveway. The skip is piled higher every morning. It contains a mattress, springs, old carpet, cardboard boxes. I don't approach.

As if the wall is an algorithm set to lure me in, today there is a little ceramic Wade figurine of a toad. Wade miniatures are like gold dust these days. Proper collectors items. At car boot sales you have to haggle with the old women, coaxing them to part with their ceramic cats. It's odd that this toad is on his own, you don't normally find them like that. I think, at one time, he must have been a gift. I turn him slowly in my hands. The skip glows yellow through the wimpy hedge. I lean against the railings, to get a better view. The toad is cold and his base is satisfyingly chinked and dimpled. There is no sign of life in the house. I think: the homeowner has certainly died.

When I get home, I put the toad on a bookshelf in my bedroom. He is gloopily glazed in khaki, with gold ringed eyes. In his newly elevated position, he takes on a distant look. His chin, slightly turned up, looking away from me. I try to imagine where the toad lived in the old man's house (I'm sure he is a man. There are indicators.) I imagine on the desk, looking up at his owner with warmth.

The toad was a special find. Most days, it's just books. I rarely take more than one home with me, but I look through them all. The books tell me more about the man than anything else. For example, there is a significant amount of medical literature. Three thin volumes on childhood epilepsy and migraines. These are stacked on top of a hefty leather clad tome on developmental neurology and, hidden beneath that, is a small ring bound book full of old school brain imaging. I sift through several mental health classification books, including an ancient stapled copy of the DSM-IV. I put this in my tote bag; I've always wanted to read it. All of these sit on the wall, better preserved than the handful of modern paperbacks with cracked spines that have been cast into a cardboard box on the pavement below. These are surely destined to be pulped.

Just as I'm beginning to lose hope in his literary taste, I find a miniature edition of *North and South*. It is languishing in the box, among the bestsellers. It is the first object that seems truly abandoned and I lift it up. It is spitting that day, and under my fingers the droplets smear across the cover making a paste from the thickly inset dust. Inside the cover are two initials in blue ink: A. R. I put it gingerly into my tote bag. For the first time, my thoughts slide to the person who is choosing which objects are sent to the wall, to the box, and which are kept inside.

I take *North and South* to the lido, making sure it is wholly covered by my bag and towel while I swim. As I breathe, push, count, one, two, three, the rain works itself up into a fury. Most of the pool clears. Fair weather swimmers. The droplets bounce off the pool surface and splash my face. An old man is one of the stoics. He shares my lane. He is slower than me and I could easily overtake him, but I find myself enjoying his partial company. His neck is turtley above the water, and his ancient mouth moves as he swims like he is suckling. I wait at each end of the pool for him to reach the opposite wall. This way, we pass each other on every traversal, acknowledging one another with a smile and our eyes lifting to the heavens. "Well, we can't get any wetter," I say. "Quite," he replies. We stand under the hot showers together and then dry ourselves. The rain glances off his bald head, which he shades with a newspaper retrieved from inside his shoes. He dresses quickly and precisely, smoothing his jumper down over his belt. I am seized by a sudden urge to ask his name. I dither for a moment, taking far too long to wiggle my swimsuit off under my t-shirt. He wishes me a good day.

The rain continues all afternoon. It pelts the window as I read *North and South* in the snug of my bed. Imagining the tissuey, elderly hands of A. R. turning the pages slowly is the closest I've felt to another person in months. The bottom corner of page twenty-three is folded. I unfold it and trace the scar with my fingers. I fold it again, scanning the page for that sentence, the one that had to be kept. I reread the page and then again. I go no further with the novel, though the page ends on *and*. I bring the book to my face and bury my nose in its seam. Mildew, dust mites, glue.

The brief enchantment of *North and South* is broken by forty-eight hours of bland reference books. European travel guides, A-Zs and dictionaries, manuals for Microsoft Office. I leave most of these, but I do smuggle away (with much effort) a five volume Encyclopaedia. I also pocket a Wisden cricket almanack. It is mustard yellow and seems never to have been opened. I rip off the note that's taped to it instructing me to enquire at the house for further copies, and pocket that too, thus singlehandedly preventing anyone else from acquiring the full set. Alongside the horses from the toy farm set, this is my most lawless act.

I am growing fond of *A*. Always, he finds ways to surprise me. The reference books are brought to a sudden end by a mug that declares him 'World's Best Dad'. I drink tea from it that evening and think how nice it would have been to grow up in that house. I fondle the plastic horses and imagine trekking them across the carpets of *A's* office, making them vault over the sudden obstacle of his shoes.

One Tuesday, faced by yet another leaning tower of medical literature, I wonder how much longer I can stand *A's* evasiveness. The books interested me to begin with, when I felt they were helping me glean an understanding of *A's* professional life, but, after two weeks of daily additions, their sheer volume is stultifying. I suspect he is using them to resist my approaches. I give them a dutiful assessment, rustling their pages with my thumb like a flip book. I nearly miss it. Hidden in a thoroughly dry two-hundred page examination of metastasis, I find a 'Property Of New College Library' stamp. The week prior, I'd lifted a framed print of New College from 1914. It was obvious that *A* was an alumnus. This breakthrough produces such a dizzying rush that I have to sit on the wall for a moment to compose myself. I commit myself to taking photographs of all the objects that I can't take away with me, in case they become vital later on.

Sitting there on the wall, the street looks different; wider. The house opposite, a mirror image of *A's*, has no hedge obscuring the railing. The front garden is sparsely gravelled, with no planting at all beyond two spindly olive trees castrated by their concrete pots. My dear *A* woke up most mornings to this view, confronted by its sterility as he shuffled to the corner shop for a newspaper. The people in the grey house must look over at his wayward hedge and ivy smocked walls, and wrinkle their noses. I place my hand on the wall and rub it gently. Behind me there is a clatter, a crunching and then the slam of a door. I whip my head round, but the door is closed again. The skip is now iced with white hospital handrails. I sigh.

The only object on the wall the following day is a black cloth-bound volume. It is heavy and the spine has been worn to gossamer thinness with opening and closing and leaving it face down with its poor pages splayed. The text is dense and divided into narrow columns. On several pages there are printed etchings of strange veined swellings, trailing umbilical cords and stern one-eyed foetuses floating in the dark. The pages are covered with fine pencilled marginalia. The kind of scribblings and furious notes that reveal something deep and private about a mind. The entirety of a first name and a date is scribbled in the front. I try googling the name in combination with medical journals and terminology and New College, Oxford. There are hundreds of embryologists called Arthur. I sift by date, going back further and further until word processing is replaced by type set and crudely scanned articles. Nothing comes up. I take out a free trial on several paywalled journals. Still nothing. I try 'Arthur' and 'Herne Hill'. I try 'Arthur', 'Scientist' and 'Obituary'. I try 'Arthur' and 'Doctor' and 'Professor' and 'Embryology'. There are thousands of results. I email the council and ask to view the open electoral register. They direct me to the local library.

Finally, here, clicking through an endless roll call on a creaking Dell computer, I find a surname. Armed with it, scribbled down on a piece of paper, I can hardly bear to google him. I bob goodbye and thanks to the librarian and scurry home. When I get back, I roll the piece of paper, hot and soft from being crushed in my hand, into a thin tube and cram it inside the belly of the toad. I do not say the name out loud. Instead, I get into bed and move the name round my mouth with my tongue. My thumb hovers over safari on my phone. I can't. Not yet. I check my email. In my inbox, amongst the spam are three emails chasing overdue blog posts. The oldest one was sent a week ago.

I notice that every day now, as well as the skip, and the books and DVDs on the wall, furniture is stacked up in the driveway in discrete piles. I watch a car drive in and claim one pile. A young couple load side tables and bookshelves into their boot, while their dog yanks aggressively on its lead and whinnies at the closed front door. I wait for a while to see if someone will come out to greet the couple, perhaps to exchange cash. Nothing. The couple reverse away, nodding at me, as if to say 'thanks for waiting'. Sat beside the lido that morning, I search gumtree and facebook marketplace for Arthur's furniture. Art deco to mid-century, most of it. I narrow my search radius to 0.2 miles. Three items listed in the last twenty-four hours. I hesitate. Only for a second. Then I send a pre-programmed message enquiring after the availability of an ergonomic desk chair; I had been meaning to get one.

After I have dried myself off and reassembled my outfit, I check my messages. Teasingly my message has been marked as seen. I click on the seller's profile, which has stringent, anally retentive privacy settings. He has a different surname to Arthur, but I know they are father and son. I'm sure of it. I click on the profile picture which is, unhelpfully, a photograph of the back of his head gazing loftily at a green mountain. His previous photos follow the same format. I think: *Relax - strangers see your face everyday.*

Walking past the house later that morning, I notice a light is on in one of the upstairs windows. I go back to my messages and draft something more personal, I hope, more tempting. Hey! This looks really ideal for me. Only thing is, I don't have a car to pick it up. *I'm based in Herne Hill. Is that walking distance/could you deliver? The ellipsis bubbles below. Are you near Herne Hill Road? Afraid I'm not doing deliveries, but the chair has wheels so you could push it along. Address is:*

The address is perfect. I look at the house, and feel a tingling warmth spreading to my fingers and toes. *It's in excellent condition. Hardly used.* I agree to collect it the following day, and to transfer thirty pounds to his PayPal account.

The chair is left out for me, beside the other trophies. It is the first time that I set foot on the driveway, beyond the jurisdiction of the wall. I knock on the door, chewing my lip with anticipation, going over what I hope to say. Thank you so much, I think I'll be fine wheeling it home, I only live over - gesture - but could you just help me get it onto the pavement because the wheels are getting stuck in the grass and gravel. No answer. I knock again. I hover for a few moments, before my phone buzzes to tell me that my swim booking starts in five. The chair is pretty easy to navigate onto the pavement and to wheel home. I put my running shoes on and sprint down the hill to the pool. In the rush, I leave my towel folded on the swivel chair and I have to air dry myself in the changing room.

On my way home, icy with the indignity of my towellessness, I spot him. The son. He is hefting carpet into the skip, grunting. He is taller than I imagined. I haven't got my glasses on me, to see the details of his face, but in soft focus they look shadowy and appealing. I can at least tell that his cheeks are red. I can see he has a beard too, though I cannot be sure how thick. This is my Arthur's own son, come to take the weight of his father's life, to measure it out in objects and make an inventory of the man. He is beautiful. I want to shout *Hey! I know you!* I just gaze at him. And when he looks up, like a deer lighting on the presence of a poacher, I gasp and slip away.

Necessarily, I have cut down on blog posts. There just isn't time. Irked by the daily requests, I email my regulars to say I'm taking a week off. To cover my rent for the month, I pitch a weekly segment to the swimsuit company, to write a blog about how swimming transforms my mental health. I ask for an advance and six weeks to prepare the first month of content. I tell them the first two weeks will be dedicated to research.

The world is always conspiring to distract me from pressing matters. At the end of my first week of research my own mother phones me. She tells me that my dad has had some bad news. She assumes I am too busy to visit him and is delighted when I say I can come immediately. I interrupt her prattling to say I will stay for the weekend.

My parents live in Brighton, in a squat brick house near a carpark in the middle of the city. On almost every surface in the house there is a small and assiduously arranged assemblage of knick knacks. My mother puts them together when she is stressed. In a way, it is a relief to be with them. They are very ordinary people. They only like to listen to the radio. When my father collects me from the station, he puts the radio on so we don't have to talk. When we get home, we sit at the table in the kitchen. I give him the 'World's Best Dad' mug, and watch him examine it carefully. It looks large in his hands, like it is shouting at him. He does not say anything but when my mother bustles in, he looks up and I spy the twinkle of tears on his lashes.

On Sunday morning, my mother and I go for a swim in the sea, while my dad sits on the pebble beach pocketing stones. We swim out until we're in line with the yellow buoy and my mother asks me if I would like to have a bath when I get back in, only she noticed last night that I didn't have one, and my hair is beginning to grease. I dip my head into the water. I hadn't noticed the stress I was under. My mother asks me whether I've been eating? How my stomach is? Whether it's been better since I came off the pill? She has more questions than a customer satisfaction survey. She begs me to let her organise a consultation with her homoeopath, and I am forced to tell her once again that I don't believe in it. She looks heartbroken and starts swimming back to shore.

In the station carpark, my dad puts his hand on my knee. He says, very slowly, "We are nearly at the end now." I know he means for me to squeeze his hand but I can't. I tell him that I love him. We have been nearly at the end for twenty years, since before my memories began. He tells me to go to the doctor if my stomach keeps hurting me. I promise I will, and let myself out of the car.

With all this travelling, I can only make the midday slot at the lido. It's much later than I like to swim. At this hour, the sun will be dazzling off the water painfully, and armfuls of babies will be squawking and splashing at the shallow end of the pool. I steel myself for this as I walk down the hill. Perhaps it's because I've been away, or perhaps it's because it's empty for the first time in weeks, I walk straight past the wall. I know this because I slam into the son as he comes out of the gate. He is wearing red swimming trunks and a green jumper, and he has a stripy towel under his arm. I apologise, keeping my eyes on my shoes. He insists it's his fault for not looking where he was going. With a furtive wave he moves off, down the hill, striding. I hang back.

He's already in the water when I arrive. I had to negotiate with the receptionist to let me in late. All the time we are swimming, him in the slow lane, me in the medium today, I keep one eye on him. He moves gracefully through the water, staying under the surface for a long time before gliding up to take a breath. He stops at the end of each length to lounge back, letting his head tilt into the sun. He even shares a giggle with a youngish mother, whose baby splashes him and he doesn't flinch. I count his lengths. Barring any surreptitiously nippy ones he got in before I arrived, I count eight. A leisurely eight. In counting his, my number has slipped from my grasp. I watch carefully as he rises out of the pool, taking the stairs. I stay crouched so that even in the shallow end only my eyes and nose are above the surface. From here, I watch him under the shower, rinsing the chlorine off, letting his hair grow sodden and slop over his face. When he has left, heading home boldly in soaking trunks, I top myself up with ten determined lengths of the fast lane.

I change my lido slot to midday for the next day too. I have a restless morning pacing my flat and checking the time. At eleven, I remove the sanitary sticker from my bikini and put it on. I dress carefully in a tight miniskirt and a floaty vest. He isn't at the pool. I swim forty lengths at pace, until my hips ache. My knees tremble when I walk home.

The wall accrues a scattering of souvenirs, but I hardly look at them now. I have a new routine. I put the bikini on each day and head to the pool at half ten. I unfold a lounger, and sit beside the pool with my legs stretched out decorously. I peer over my laptop and scan the pool for red shorts. I send the marketing manager a suggestion for the title of the first blog; How a red swimsuit improves your confidence, the science. I purchase a cappuccino and a croissant from the cafe and eat it slowly, peeling the layers of the pastry apart and dipping them in the coffee. I swim, and then I wait, and then I swim again. I rinse the chlorine off and take to carrying a travel pot of moisturiser to revive my skin. When the pool becomes too clogged with small children, I walk back to the flat. I stop for a few minutes to look through the railings of Arthur's house. I imagine him inside packing his father's study into boxes, or perhaps unpacking his own things onto his father's shelves.

When we finally bump into each other again, my heart skitters like I'm meeting a celebrity. I am instantly dispossessed of language, barely able to make my eyebrows jump in that way that says "It's you."

He is on his way to the lido. He is wearing his green jumper and I notice now that he has gnawed holes in the sleeves so he can stick his thumbs through. He looks at me with a widening smile. It is excruciating to be so close to him and yet I cannot ask the things I want to know. Or hint at the drawer of objects I've snuck away, nor the photos I've taken. I can't demonstrate how close I've got to knowing him, how tantalisingly near I am. That I have now googled his father several times, just to read the articles and draw a line to the books that were once piled up on this wall. Research is not as rewarding as imagination, but right answers are right answers no matter how you get them. I think about kissing him there, just to have something to do. Instead, I say: "I bought a chair from you."

"Did you?" The bemused cocking of his head loosens his curls and one winds its way down his nose. "Well, I picked it up from this house." He nods in slow realisation. "Sorry, yes. Huge clear out." He indicates the overflowing skip, "Hard to keep track of it all - " He clearly thinks I'm nuts. I put my hand through my hair casually, then retract my hand in case it looks like an anxious tick. "I noticed." He makes a schoolboy face at me. Then he gestures at my towel, poking out of the tote bag. "Are you headed to the lido?" I nod. He lifts up his own towel sympathetically. "Shall we walk?"

Only when we are walking beside each other and our faces are parallel, do I rustle up the chutzpah to suggest we get a coffee afterwards. He says: "I've never gone on a date with someone I met online." I say: "Hardly met! You didn't even come outside to help me lug the bloody thing out of the driveway." That makes him laugh, and then it's easy.

I am wearing my bikini, even though it is now September and the sun has largely faded from the sky. It clings and squeezes every essential part of my figure. Arguably, a perfect design.

I resist the urge to put my hair up. We keep talking as we descend into the water. He rubs his hands together, wriggles his shoulders and makes odd chirping noises to show how frisk it is. I am silent, smiling at the back of his head, longing to reach out and stroke the duck tail at the nape of his neck.

I swim breaststroke with him in the slow lane. I coil my arms in and tuck my heels right up near my groin, then unleash them all, springing forward, like a frog. He swims gently, just behind me. I turn onto my back to swim facing him. This slows me down, which means I don't lose him. We keep our heads above water and chat. After four lengths like this, I feel the urge to kick away, sharpish. I say I might do a few quick lengths in the other lane. He smiles obliquely. When I return, the slow lane has been usurped by toddlers and he is nowhere to be seen.

I wait outside the lido, telling myself that we agreed to go for coffee. We did agree. He said it was a date. I think about slipping away. Another person looks me up and down as they walk past. The humiliation is too hard to take. I tug at my jeans' waistband, trying to hitch them up higher, snugger round my arse. I feel my heart whir behind my ribs as the time passes. Finally, he comes through the turnstile. "Ah there you are. I was waiting inside at the cafe for ages. I thought we were getting a coffee?"

My cheeks flush and my eyes prick. He looks at me. "Do you want to go to Sesami? I fancy one of those spinach borek things." He begins to walk away with an easy, swaggering grace, turning his head at last to look at me. "Come on then."

As we walk away from the lido, he tells me how nice it is to live near a swimming pool, like he has just discovered it all over again. He says "of course, *you* know" like we are the only people who really go to the lido. I think about the fair weather swimmers with distaste and place him in the same category as me, the long term committed. I think about how Arthur must have taught him how to swim, holding his body up with his hands. I think about pushing him over onto the tarmac of the road so I can pull his t-shirt up to kiss his soft white belly. I walk slightly behind him all the way to the café, and think about his skin under my lips.

He tells me over scalding coffee in paper cups that he is doing a PhD in developmental neurology. He tells me that there are so many factors that affect in utero brain development and we've only just scraped the surface. The womb environment really is the 'third way' in the nature/nurture dichotomy. I nod. I want to say *just like your father*. Instead, I eat my borek and sip my coffee, though it sears my gums. He chats away like there is nothing simpler in the world than saying what you think. Eventually, noticing my silence, he asks me: "How are you finding the chair?" I smile: "It's exactly what I wanted."

Later, we will be lying in bed naked beside each other in my flat. I will observe how surprisingly small his feet are. High arches, thin toes. He will observe that I am odd. Quiet. I never ask questions. As he speaks, he will turn the ceramic toad over in his hands. My ears will pink with fear about his father's name stuffed inside it. I tell myself that it's alright. He seems happy.

But it is strange. The way he looks at it like he's never seen it before in his life.

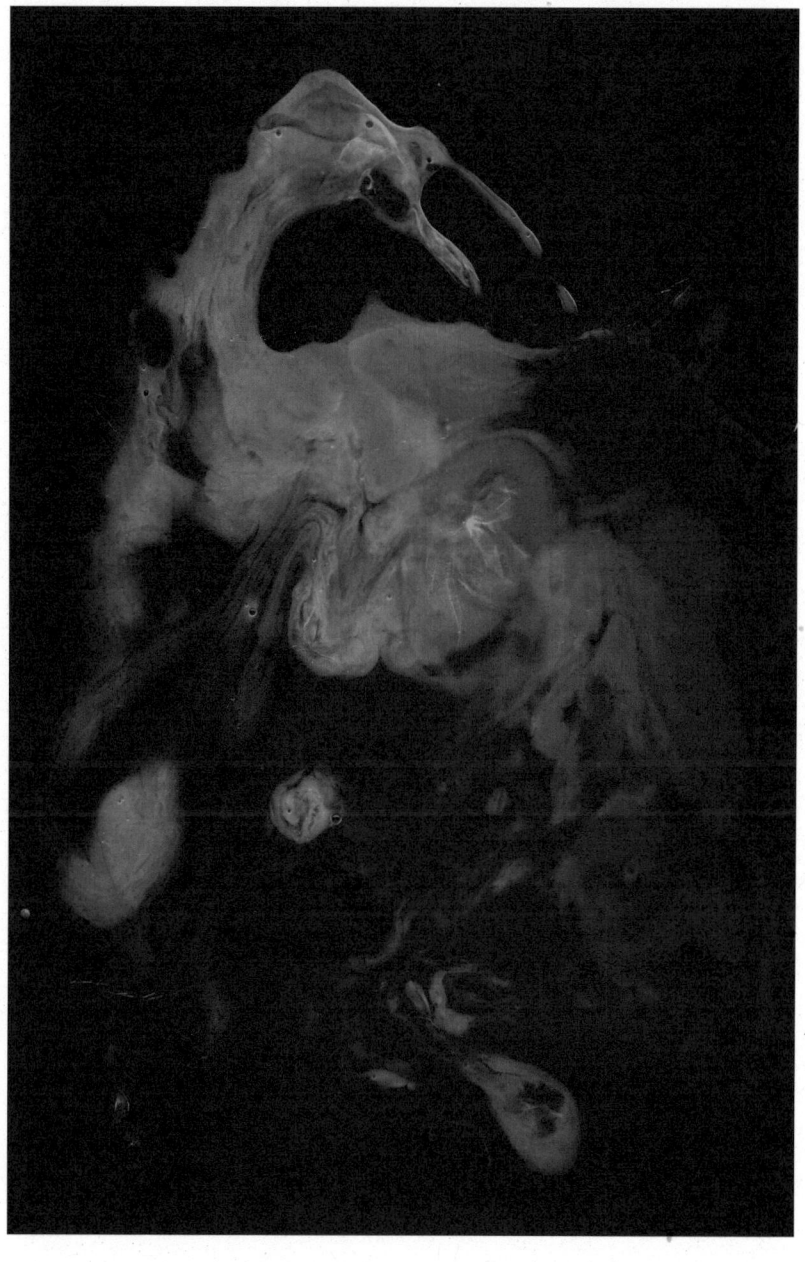

this is the season
male bees are thrown
out of the hive

It is hard to imagine how their bodies will look without clothes
how their stomachs might collapse in against their hips or stick
out round and pronounced and either way the skin might be loose
and fleshy or taut that they might be little and surreptitious or
huge and arrogant and they might be flecked all over with spots
they might be covered in long black hairs or only a tuft in the
middle of the sternum and another below their navel and their
heads might seem too small or too large and they might seem
shorter than me or taller and I might think they are pleasant to
look at or look away or more often than not not think of it at
all and only notice how strong they are when they push into me
and I start to realise that I will never say no but I will think as I
lie there acquiescing that I prefer men that make me feel fragile
men that might break me so I can fight back and bite and bruise
them but all of it is not quite violence

One day I think I will marry a brute and be unhappy and
unsatisfied but I will know we are fucking because I will feel
the weight of him like a breeze block on my pelvis and that will
centre me and I will know that my body is real and I will know
that we are both in the room and I will feel like I can throw
things at him and growl and hiss and he will make me cry and

we will eat each other and spit each other out and I will want to impress him and he will not be impressed and I will be repulsed by him but I will not pity him and that is why I will be able to speak and that is as close as I will come to love

All this I think while still you labour over me

You feel so much smaller than me I spend the whole night worrying that I will roll over and smother you like mothers do with their babies sometimes but that is not fair because you are not small really you are a few inches taller than me probably taller than my father I lift my head a little from the pillow to assess your height from the ripple of your vertebrae between your shoulders rising from the mattress hunched as you are at the end of the bed between my split legs five eleven and a half I guess though aren't you all always?

The great human endeavour to be marginally taller than your parents producing generations of stretched necks balancing books and anxiously carving notches onto door frames to say I used to be here and now I am higher until we are all so bored that we think of our fathers without kink while we fuck each other and I just feel so old nowadays and so bored that lying on my back like this I feel like a hefty bee her legs twitching as she is suckled at by a nervous worker and this is the season that male bees are thrown out of the hive

By she the bumble queen in her mohair regalia practising mindfulness pushing raisins round her cheeks to stay present until her whole self is so inexorable from that moment that she must simply die of exhaustion all life happening at once in one instant until she combusts in a puff of yellow pollen and I sneeze

Your face slightly startled rises over the hillock of my pubis and smiles worthily so I simper extend my hands and invite you to nestle against my chest and you drool a little though don't you all always?

I struggle not to inventory the times that I have lain this way before the list of biro scratched names in the back of my teenage diary starting at eleven in joined up letters with a blue fountain pen carefully recording one after another first and last names until I am seventeen and suddenly the names are first names accented with question marks and notable facial features like moles trickle of ellipsis that represent a whole spectrum of tender lads from the most handsome old fashioned Caravaggio cherub to the boniest froggiest chapped lipped boy on the bus across the bridge and the one with the strict jewish parents who made me sleep in a separate room lightly dreaming til he came creeping up the stairs squeak by squeak and then the gawky bright eyed too much talking taught muscled adolescent in New York who used to text me the registration of a cab and I climb in and zip through the city in dirty knickers to see him in the flat with the cats that belonged to this aunt who might come back so I couldn't sleep there and I'd shrug secretly relieved and slip off into the night and dive headfirst into a gaggle of young men and plough right through wan and confused and cerebral and at the furthest reach of my teens where they have turned into my twenties last week that truly sleek young man with a beautiful face and surly demeanour who bought me dinner and wore a ring on his pinky finger but still he had like they all have something of that brittleness around the eyes a nervousness in the mouth and the texture of his skin rough and fuzzy fraught with apology that they have tricked me into thinking I wanted to fuck them when all I wanted to do was sit close to them and talk until the sun rose above the roofs of whichever famous city in that washed out light I always find myself too polite too embarrassed to refuse their earnest pricks and still now I know it means nothing when I commit myself to never again sleeping with a man that seems as submerged by his own growth as you

When we were friends before all this I used to tease you and you'd laugh with me when I told you about all of them every single one that traipsed out of my bedroom in the early morning bedraggled and alone carrying their jumpers and jackets like babes in arms and we laughed at them together so you knew my blank face my run a bath and lie in it til my fingers prune my hand lingering on the kettle my glance up glazed eye sorry where was I

You knew that it was not for want of trying

I was making you laugh last night with running commentary on adjacent strangers' conversations and crabbing my hand behind a man's back and making snide remarks in earshot always about estate agents' lack of taste and you snatched my hand and hid it beneath the table so when the man turned round twice we saw in his eyes that he had conflicting feelings about his grip on reality and it felt nice you holding my hand and giggling and I wanted to talk to you alone all night but one of our vague friends kept sidling over and tapping you on the shoulder asking if you wanted to come to bathroom for a bump and you kept shrugging him off maybe latering and swinging your big wet eyes back to me and that felt very very nice and so then I decided I should try it try you on for size

How it happens is that I decide and then my will that singular instinct is sent out into the ether and no longer mine to recall until I find myself pinned against a wall or a hand in my hand or a shared cab and I don't really want to but I decide I have to go through with it just to see if I can to amass a little more data to better establish the boundaries of my body because I want to know that I could can mould them like putty in my palm that I can make them yelp and grow heavy that I can make them sleepy and soft and that at the crest of it just before that paroxysm of pleasure I can render them desperate and clutching and lost in the world

It was irresponsible to employ the same methods, and expect different results

As my best friend told me once when I was weeping in the bath I spend my life wishing people were psychic and then getting pissed off that they weren't she thought that was unfair but I said not psychic but sensitive she just rolled her eyes and I sank my head under the water until my chest felt like it was going to cave in and I had to rupture the surface soaking her trouser leg which dripped steadily onto the tiles to clarify I don't like to say things out loud that's all I'm one of those people who will text someone even if they're sitting in the same room or I'll walk off in an argument to draft a paragraph in my notes because I have all these full sentences in my head that I just can't get out and it's not a very sustainable approach I know but I don't think it applies here anyway because I'm hardly going to pause at the critical moment when your cock's hanging out to just draft a quick message something pithy and professional like let's take a rain check

So I keep my lips slightly parted so you can kiss them

And my eyes stay open looking at you all the time when you walk your fingers down below my navel and I say stop my voice is strangled and you whisper soothingly I'm just touching like you know and your voice is all gentleness and the taste of smoke and you have this tender way of insisting but don't you all always?

Such an innocent you are incredulous as a child explaining to a baffled parent why despite the years wide gap in life experience they in fact are right and I am swept with this rising revulsion this which I can barely contain and my brain seems to lift out of my body as easily as jelly schloops out of its silicone mould and my body is left gaping and unstuffed and I hover above myself humming my wings thrumming the air and I look down at her and

I throw myself against the glass once twice –

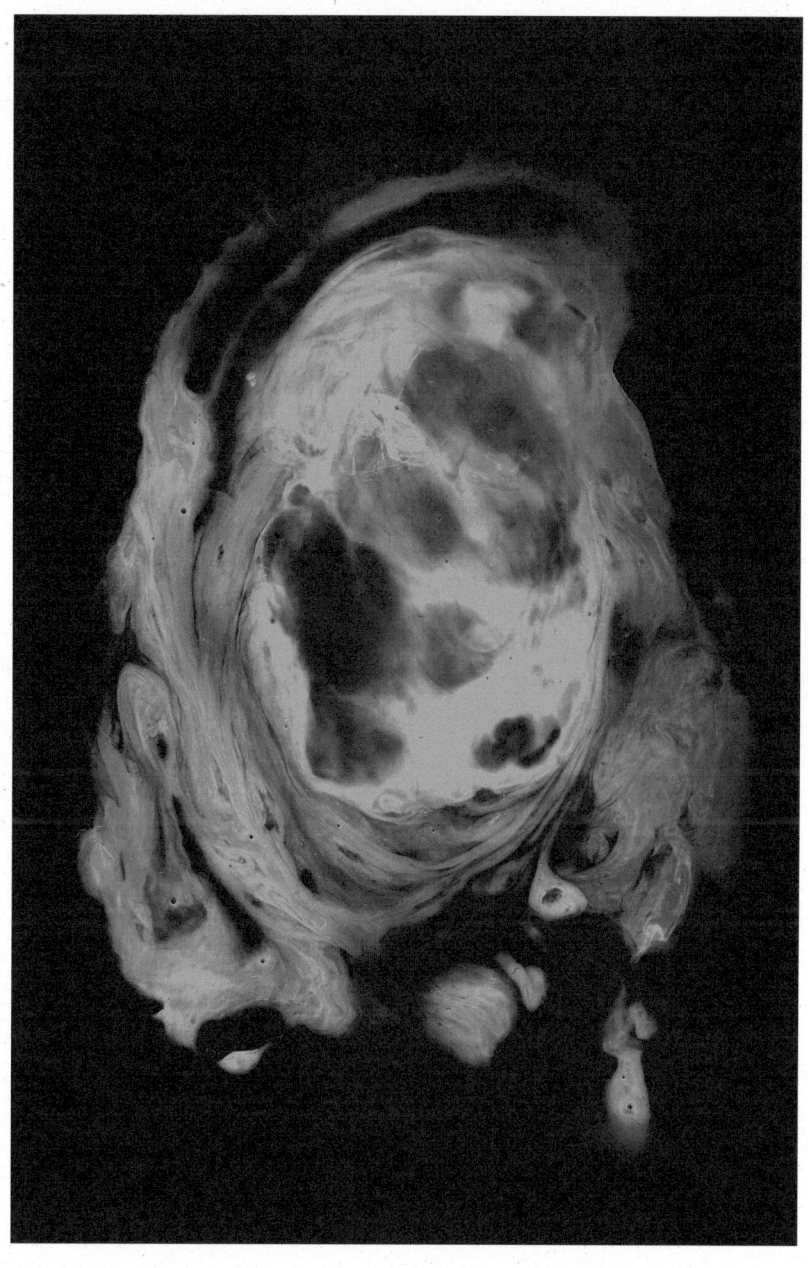

Now Their Necks
Are Cracked

The woods lie in quiet wait. For weeks they have been turning, shifting, the thin trees quickening too eagerly into leaf. Beneath the canopy, the bluebells have sucked the last moisture from the earth, their spindle white roots worming into the dirt. Every day the news reporter says it is the driest April on record. We have not noticed because we only notice the weather when it is wet. We hate wearing raincoats so much that we gave mine away to a charity shop. It is the Easter before our exams begin. We are seventeen.

You pick me up from the station in your aunt's car. The back seat is slippery with receipts and magazines which you push to one side to clear a seat for me. My heel sinks into a discarded coke can with a crunch. I lean my cheek against the window glass. Driving lessons were your seventeenth birthday present from your mother. You were pleased. You kept saying that when you got your licence we could go on long drives, to France maybe, or maybe you'll just come back to London whenever you want. The flush of adventure ebbed when you realised practise meant driving to the supermarket every Saturday while your mother dug her fingers into the dashboard and prayed under her breath. Now the thing is turning eighteen, so you can get your own car. You are working in a Spar to save up.

Your big cousin, Otis, is here. Barely a year older than you, rarely mentioned in our phone calls, but he's got a licence so "he counts." Those were the words you said into my ear as you unfurled my fingers from the handle of my suitcase and hefted it down the station steps. In the passenger seat in front of me, I can see the furred edge of Otis' cheek silhouetted against the rushing motorway. He's got dark hair that snakes over his shoulders and a stretcher in his ear. He drums his fingers on the dashboard, pouting at himself in the wing mirror. I decide to hate him because he is hogging the passenger seat, where I should be. Beyond his head rest, I sneak tail flicking looks at you. Intent focus scrunches your nose, sniffing for hazards to the left, right, ever ahead. Your eyes resist following your chin as you turn your head slightly and ask me, "Are you excited?" Otis snorts. Your eyes leave the road now, briefly. I am flushed with embarrassment for both of us.

The road we take is a red artery on the sat nav. An avenue of trees drops us suddenly into shadow. The road carves through the land, a deep ditch and rising banks of browning bracken on either side. An aluminium sign indicates an upcoming fork in the road. The fork is steeper than the sign suggested, almost doubling back on itself. You feed the wheel furiously, swinging the car to the right. I tense my knees and press my hips firmly into the seat to avoiding sliding across the backseat, with the magazines.

"Nicely done," Otis nods approvingly.

I notice his knuckles are white, gripping the edge of his seat. You sigh, straightening up, and look over your shoulder at me, smiling. I look at the silver ring winking on your pinky finger. You have beautiful hands. They are slender, with pronounced veins. You turn your eyes back to the road.

A deer leaps out of the bracken, just ahead. You break. The eyes strain from its head. The breaks shriek. The weight of the car, as it careers down the potholed lane, is immense. The deer skitters on its hooves in ballet pose, its huge eyes flashing. The car jolts forward. The deer leaps back into the undergrowth, which is the same colour as its coat. I am thrown forwards, knocking my chin on Otis' headrest. I slam my hand onto the window, feeling my skin tugging on the glass. You pant. You take your hands off the wheel and hold them up. Otis breaks the silence with a single, spit-filled "fuck."

You drive on silently. I watch your hands again, squeezing the wheel and then releasing.

We drive slowly into the woods. All around us the ground is flooded with bluebells. Otis jumps out to unlock the gate and holds it open like a guard to let the car pass. I feel his eyes on me through the glass as I take my chance to reach forward and squeeze your shoulder. I say: "Do you think they'll like me?" You nudge your cheek against my wrist.
"They're all really nice." I sit back in my seat, slightly deflated. I wanted to be told that I was, or was sure to be, loved.

Otis loads my arms with bags and pushes me towards the fire pit. I step into the clearing and make a brief assessment of your new friends. They form the periphery of the popular circle. This much is clear from the quality of their pubescent skin. They are minute keepers; non-smokers; late braces; virgins; reserves, available to be substituted in when the inner clique becomes smothered by its own incestuousness. The girls form a Midgard serpent, sitting between each other's legs, fiddling with their thin knotted ankle bracelets and plaiting each other's hair. One of them breaks the chain to twist around and peer at me. She stretches her sleeve around her fist and glances furtively through her eyelashes. I am wearing dungarees that I have cut off too high up my thigh. I feel her register this. You appear from behind me.

"Finn!" she cries and sounds the alarm to the boys, chins pinked with shaving rash, who wrestle over which of them will tackle you to ground first. They pile on. You cough, bellow and struggle, digging your elbow into their chests. As boys do, they shout the moves as they administer violence. Satisfied, they peel off you one by one. The last boy straddles you, holding you on the ground, and only loosens his grip when you admit finally that he has won. He ruffles your hair affectionately and turns round to look at me. He looks up at my legs, down at you, back to my legs. When you are finally allowed to stand up, your jumper stretched and your new nikes brown with dust, you introduce us.

"This is Ralph."

You steer me round the circle, reciting the names. I let them wash over me. "Daisy" blushes when you point at her; I smile my nicest smile. The other girls look straight past you, and stare hawkishly at me instead. When we complete the circle, Ralph is waiting. He is by far the largest and most developed of the boys, with a few dark hairs stubbornly sprouting from his top lip and between his eyebrows. He presents a hand for me to shake. His palm is moist in mine, and calloused like an older man's. Smiling from just one side of his mouth, he seems to speak for the group when he says: "We've heard a lot about you." I can't say the same.

Last summer, you moved here. To "The Middle of Nowhere". You call it Otherland, Oafland, Outback, Arse end, Sweet Suburbia, Sydenham-on-sea, this pissing place, this dump, this hole. Your mother calls it paradise. She calls it our corner of the island. She calls it home. I call it Finnbar's, now.

It took you weeks to pack your things up into brown boxes salvaged from the street. Eating dinner in hostile silence, ignoring the Dulux colour charts your mother unfurled on the table. You slammed doors in her face, and behind those same doors, you lay on the floor examining old football cards. I rubbed your back, and promised to keep things under my bed for you. In the evenings you snuck away from the house to smoke loose rollies in my garden. Your spit couldn't get the paper to stick. I used my nails to roll tight, thin cigarettes, to stretch the baccy further. I roll one now as I settle myself on a log. Back then, we'd be sat on the concrete garden steps, you mumbling glumly while I picked snails off the bricks. We clinked bottles and you toasted my parents. My house is always free. There is always a pouch of tobacco on the side and beers in the fridge. My parents never complain about noise or mess. Once, you got too drunk and went staggering up the garden path to piss, whistling my father's praises all the way. Then a splash. You looked so shocked, standing knee deep in the garden pond. I laughed and you stamped off, slamming the front door, leaving a trail of swampy footprints in your wake. When you knocked later, and I answered, your eyes didn't open. You only parted your lips to ask, "Can I stay?"

While you catch up with everyone, I grab the tent bag and look for a space to put it up. I choose a sparse bluebell patch within a ring of creaking birch trees. I use the side of my shoe to drag and kick sticks and leaves away. Your mother has lent us the family four-man tent for Otis, you and I to share. I shake it out. It is unwieldy large and spotted with mildew. Your mother warned that Otis had used it last at a festival in the summer. I wrangle its skin onto the poles. When it's up, I zip myself in. I sweep the groundsheet with my hands, gathering up old sweet wrappers, a few lost swan filters and the foil corner of a condom packet. I tip the debris into the net pocket by the door. I hug my knees to my chest. *Come and find me, come and find me, come and find me.* The minutes drag.

When I emerge back into the woodland, the sky is turquoise. I weave back to the fire site, narrowly dodging a green apple that smashes in front of my feet. I look up. A rambunctious grey squirrel is bouncing on a branch, biting into them, wincing and then lobbing them onto a growing mound of sweetly rotting fruit. In the distance I can see you, and all your friends, harassing each other. As I approach, standing on the edge for a while, rubbing my arm, you break out from the swill, out of breath and put your arm round my neck. You squeeze me. You say you missed me, you miss me all the time. It is like ribbons the way you talk, tying me up.

As you drag me off down the path, I look back over my shoulder at the group, until they disappear behind a bramble. The path grows narrower and narrower until it is little more than a muddy vein, trampled with deer tracks. Panting, I ask you to slow down. You run faster.

"Look!" you come to an abrupt stop.
"What?" I say, still chasing my breath. Your two forefingers find the nook under my chin, and tilt my head upwards. I had not realised I had spent the entire walk staring vigilantly at the ground in case of roots that would unbalance me. In front of us is the huge exposed root structure of a fallen tree. A shaggy mess of ochre clay clods and dangling threads emanate from a triad of talon like major roots. The trunk itself is smooth, dry and white, like a bone. It has been thoroughly gnawed and

stripped of bark by deer. A huge crater has been gouged from the earth where the roots once were. Its walls are run with holes like a colander. You get on your knees and hang your head over the edge, peering into one of the tunnels. You shout into it, then press your ear against the hole, hoping to hear an echo or the scrabbling of small paws.

I stand awkwardly above you, casting a shadow across your back. A breeze rustles the dead roots. Every cell of my body feels suddenly raw. This tree is dead, I think, this is a grave. I tap your back and you hasten to your feet.

"Can we go back to the fire?"

"I think there's rabbits in there."

"Is that why the tree fell?" My voice croaks, and I sound more mournful than I mean to.

You look at me searchingly, "Because of the warren?" We don't speak for a moment. We stare down into the crater.

"Shall we go back?" I say, eventually.

"No, let's stay here for a bit." I don't protest, even though this place gives me the heebie-jeebies. Taking the lead, you climb onto the old tree's trunk. You help pull me onto it too. It seems higher from up here than it did when we stood beside it.

"I wonder when it fell."

"Last summer," you shrug, "it was as dry as this. Loads of trees came down." You speak like you have lived here forever. I see you here in fifty years, stooping for a handful of soil to rub between your fingers.

"It nearly splatted a dog walker." I cough in shock, ashamed to laugh. You beam at me toothily. You whistle and your thumb rises through the air. Then your thumb changes course and rushes down towards your crotch. The pitch of the whistle changes.

"What a way to go," I say, drily. We swing our legs. The wood creaks.

I rest my head on your shoulder. I tell you that I've missed you. I ask about your school. I ask about the girls who are still shirking my gaze. You tell me that I mustn't take it personally. "I didn't even complain yet." You roll your eyes at me.
"Don't be like that." I redden.
You put it all down to shyness, insisting, "They are really nice when you get to know them." I scowl at you. Your face is so close to mine. My hand is resting, upturned, on your thigh. I think about squeezing you.
Instead, I poke you in the belly twice and mimic you cruelly: "Ooh, when you get to *know* them."
"Fuck off." You grab my wrist. My pointing finger dangles like a grub.
"You should speak to Daisy. She's actually really sound." I make a face. You push my shoulder hard to punish me and I topple backwards. I try to grab at the tree trunk but it is slippery and polished. I glimpse the ground below me rushing up to meet my head, and I imagine the crunch of my vertebrae stretching backwards and then slucking together like a slinky.

Just in time, your hands grab my hips and hold me fast. I hang there, my fingers trailing on the ground. I heft myself back upright using your shoulders for leverage. You wrap your arms around my waist. Our chests heave in time. My spit tastes metallic when I swallow.

Everyone is busy erecting their tents when we get back. Everywhere I look there are legs and bums protruding from creased tarpaulins and the muffled sound of squabbling elbows.

194

Otis is the only person at the fire site. He takes your shoulders in his hands and guides you conspiratorially to the edge of the wood, out into the field. I trail behind. Otis crouches down. In a fairy ring, mushrooms are growing. They are not much taller than the grass, but he parts the blades to show you their grey pointed caps and bendy stems. He asks if you know what they are and you are confident, delivering your answer back to me, "Magic mushrooms". I parrot it back to Otis.

"Psilocybin," he says, and strokes them lightly with his fingertips.

"Shall we pick some?" I ask tentatively, and reach my fingers forward to touch them. I've never tried them. I worry too much about having a bad trip, imagining spiders crawling all over my body or a fish laying eggs in my belly. You explain to me, proudly, that Otis dries them at home. I nod, still fingering one of them. Otis is squatted next to me. The damp heat of his breath behind my ear, tickles when he asks, "Have you tried them before?" I shake my head. He plucks one with ease. Then another. Folding each one into a wad of kitchen roll and tucking it into his pocket.

Bodies emerge from the newly erected tents, one after another like ants. They disappear again as quickly in search of kindling, firewood, matches. You call everyone over to help shift a pile of decent logs you have found, piling long, slime-bottomed branches on our outstretched arms. Daisy hovers around you but winces from the logs themselves. She whispers something so you bring your ear closer to her mouth. She scoops her blonde hair over her shoulder to expose her neck. You examine a possible bite. You shrug. She looks disappointed when you suggest that she helps me carry a particularly long branch over to the fire site. I hate you for that too. I have to walk backwards, head over one shoulder. She is walking slowly and I tug the branch to encourage her. She stumbles, catching her ankle on a root. The branch thumps out of our arms, onto the path. Squatting to lift it again, I raise my eyebrows at her. She laughs with relief saying, "I almost sprained my ankle." I tell her she should do up her laces. I want to shove her into a deep pile of mulching leaves. When the long branch is deposited, I sit on one end of it and roll a fag. She perches on a camping chair, a few paces from me. The air bristles.

All through the construction of the measly fire and the paltry lunch of hummus, pitta and crisps, I winch a distance between you and Daisy. I tap you on the shoulder, bringing up old jokes and people from school, but your strained laugh tells me this no longer interests you. Daisy asks if there is any tea left in the flask. I tell her to make tea if she wants it. I feel like a big territorial swan.

I ask you to come for a piss with me, dragging you away from the group. I squat behind a bush while you guard me. You tell me that you kissed Daisy at a party. I say she is pretty. You come round the side of the bush and stand in silence for a moment. I am pulling up my knickers, tangling myself in my dungaree straps.

"She told everyone she nearly choked on my tongue." Your cheeks go red even now. That would be your first kiss, I think.

"She was probably just embarrassed."

"Well, *that* makes me feel better." You cross your arms across your chest.

"Not embarrassed about *you*," I falter, "just embarrassed." You still seem put out so I say: "She clearly likes you."

"What's that face for?"

"It's fine."

"Can you stop being weird?" Your eyes on me now are so direct, peeling the skin away from my face.

"I told her you were nice."

"Shall I kiss her too, is that what you want?" You shrug and then stalk off. I follow after you, almost losing myself down rabbit holes, twice.

After lunch, you herd us all down to the lake to swim. We bound over the hill, beyond the edge of the woods where the trees grow sparser and sparser until they give in to meadow and then the lake. The grass snaps and crackles under our feet. Daisy and another girl link arms. Daisy presents her spare arm to me and I take it. We skip, knees almost hitting our chins. Otis strides past, plunges his head between our cheeks and whispers into Daisy's ear, "There are snakes in the brambles." She shrieks and we break apart. Otis strolls through the breach, smirking. When Daisy pulls me back to her she squeezes my arm and says between panting breaths, "He's so hot." I watch his bare shoulders, flexing, as he swaggers away.

The lake is brown with clay and silt, and frilled at the edges with young reeds. The sun warbles on its surface. There are rumours of fish in the lake, ancient fish. Huge, bottom feeders with whiskers, silky tails and grey, pulsing gills. They move slowly, sweeping up the mud, like priests parading the aisle. I smooth my swimming costume over my belly, hug my arms around myself and make my slow and squeamish descent. Reddish clay squelches between my toes. I think of leeches, and wish I hadn't. The boys in their long patterned swimming trunks clamber in with enthusiasm. Daisy dips a toe, retracts. Ralph strips down to his boxers. He eyes Daisy, then takes a run up and shoves her in. She thrashes beneath the surface, eventually spluttering up, incensed. I slide into the water and swim over to her. Her eyes are red and streaming. I look up at Ralph. His back is to the water now. His arms punch the air in celebration. I put my finger on my lips and beckon Daisy over to the edge where we wait, like two crocodiles, just our eyes shimmering above the surface. We each take a leg and yank. The splash wrinkles the lake.

He clambers out, and throws himself immediately back in, clownishly. I swim away from him, and all the boyish whoops of "Look at this, look at me". You are still stood on the bank. I study your strange bony feet, your hairy toes. You are pale bellied, coated in fine lanugo that glistens in the sun when you strip off your t-shirt, sheepish as your elbows get tangled in the seams and the cotton is stretched over your face. Finally, you hold your blue striate arms aloft, your palms clapping together as you prepare to dive.

Soon everyone, even Daisy, is playing at throwing themselves in, climbing out, jumping in again. I don't like getting my face wet much so I just meander around in the water, swimming vague lengths. Otis swims up beside me. He grabs my feet. I whinny and swim away. He pretends to be a shark, the way my dad used to at the swimming pool. I giggle, struggling to swim and laugh at the same time without swallowing water. I spit it up, wipe my mouth with my arm, and tell him to stop, the way you beg when you are being tickled. He turns onto his back and floats away. I tread water limply, suddenly cold.

I shimmy out of my swimsuit, make-shifting a tent with my towel. The other girls pull their jeans over their bikini bottoms, tie their jumpers around their waists. By comparison, I feel frumpy, prudish. A green prickle on my neck, behind my ears. I snatch a glance over my shoulder and I see you looking, past the knot of boys who are engaged in smearing mud on each other's backs, straight at me.

I kneel down in the mud beside the fire pit, where all the efforts from lunch have fizzled away. I begin arranging a pyre of kindling and dry thumb-thick sticks. Ralph, with toddler's impatience, suggests dowsing all the wood in vodka, or lynx, or setting fire to a tampon. The rich, solvent scent mingled with wet jeans that emanates from him as he looms over me makes me nauseous. I tuck a match into the heart of my assemblage and watch the flames tease and swell inside the chamber. I make my thumb and forefingers into a tight square hole and blow through it. The sticks glow orange, white; the flames double in size. I add more sticks and blow again. I ask for more short logs. Otis saws through the big branch that Daisy and I carried. The saw pants, huh, huh, huh. He piles the logs beside me. I take deep breaths before I blow into the fire again. Turn my face away from the smoke to breathe again. Huh. Huh. Ralph slips off, sidling up to Daisy, offering her a swig of vodka. When the fire is blazing, I rise onto my feet.

We stand at the edge of the woods and watch the sun beginning to slide away like a ball of ice-cream off a cone. Daisy asks: "Does that mean we're facing west?" We chorus: "Yes." All of us are arranged like standing stones, related by our distance from one another. You are beside me, and our eyes find each other once, twice, each time I feel a hot-cheeked sadness spreading. It's the same burgeoning grief as I felt in the tent earlier. All these years, I've felt you were my golem, made from the same clay, but now, exposed in the wide sky of this nowhere place, I see your separate body. Next year, we might not be in the same country. We might not talk at all. I swallow, frown at the setting sun, and try to focus. But I am breathless with my want of you. I look away into the woodland we have come from. It is only at this hour, when the sky is striped lilac and lucozade, that the bluebells suddenly glow. A sea of humming cerulean that stings my eyes.

As the group wanders back to the fire, slipping back into old formations, you catch my arm and hold me back in the field. We just stand there, still, and I ache. It should be natural to kiss you, now.

Instead, I am left stricken when you slip away to piss.

I make a fuss about putting our stuff in the tent before dinner. Otis, remarking crudely on the prospect of your morning glory, blithely claims the car. I wince but think that I detect relief in the twitching of your cheek. I wonder if you and Otis had agreed this, before I arrived.

Beside each other, we unroll our sleeping bags. I hook a lamp to the roof of the tent. We choose fat jumpers to wear for warmth. You lie on your back, looking up at me, while I unbuckle my dungarees to tuck my jumper in. Your eyes, trailing. The light in the tent is membranous green. I lie down beside you. It is utterly quiet, except for our breathing. You take my hand, place it on your stomach. You draw a circle on my palm, up my arm. My fingers flinch.

"I don't like Daisy, by the way," you whisper. I hold my breath, "I just wanted you to know." In my ear, these words glisten and curl, dropping off the spoon in perfect quenelles. I turn to face you. You look at me, hard. Your eyes as blue as the woodland is now. We exhale into a kiss, which tastes like pond on my lips. Your mouth is wetter than I imagined. The groundsheet crackles. I want to keep you here, as close as this. Your eyes are closed. I keep mine closed too, trying to focus on the taste of you, but my thoughts keep slipping, glitching. A weird vision of a heaving, rutting body, and some stranger face crackles in my brain like static. I hold your face in my hands. This is what I want. I shiver. You open your eyes, pull back and examine my face. My cheeks are drained of blood.

"Are you ok?" I nod. You smile.

"Brighid -" you go to say - but instead, "We should go back to the fire."

You march urgently away from me to talk to Ralph and the other boys. I fondle the bluebells with my fingertips. Otis taps me on the shoulder. His eyes narrow, and he shoots a brief look at you.

"I'm going to the shop; do you want to come?" I nod. It is the first time that day that I have needed space.

Otis loads the boot with crates of beer and two bottles of the cheapest battery acid vodka money can buy. He offers me a petrol station doughnut from a paper bag and we smoke cigarettes by the side of the road. He twirls his cigarette between his fingers, asking casually, "Do you and Finn ever -" I shake my head voraciously.

"We're friends." He shrugs.

"Doesn't mean you don't fuck each other." He inhales and digs something grey out from under his nail, "I bet he thinks about it all the time." I breathe in. I need to wee, I notice. I look vaguely for a loo but decide to wait.

"I doubt it."

"He'd never go through with it," he pauses. Sucking on his cigarette, he gives me a look, "He wouldn't want to sully you."

"I'm not a virgin," I blurt. Otis looks at me, his eyes green and flickering in the last light. He sniggers.

"That's a lie." I stand up, ruffled. Blood beats in my cheeks. On this exposed verge of the road, the wind is brisk and even through my jumper my nipples harden.

"You're a prick, you know." He smirks and shrugs again and I want to press my hands down so hard on his shoulders that his bones crumble to dust. I want to rip his mouth off his skull and stamp it into the dirt. Instead I just growl that I'm cold and he pats my head like a dog and we drive back in silence.

I don't wait for Otis to unload the boot. I walk briskly away from him to the fire, that has dwindled again in my absence. Daisy shivers beside it, swamped in a jumper I recognise. I kneel beside her and start to breathe into the embers. I rise onto my haunches and search the shadows for an idle boy who could gather wood. A phone torch swings across the fire site. You emerge behind it, some way up the path that leads to the car. Otis is with you. You both carry crates of beer. Otis is speaking, right into your ear. Your face has turned exam white. I catch your eye and wave you over. I try to smile, lovingly. You come to sit beside me and I ask, "All ok?" Otis plunks a can of beer beside me, his breath lifting the hairs on my neck.

I take it on myself to make cheese toasties on a cast iron pan even though it is now pitchy dark and the heat singes the hair on my arms. The smoke stings my eyes and in my blindness, all the bread becomes charred and carcinogenic. Still the cheese is salty and molten and oozing. The boys juggle them into their mouths, with rabid pleasure. The girls agree to split them in half, and pick at the burnt cheese round the edge with their fingernails. Otis smuggles a handful of Magic mushrooms into my pocket and tells me to put them into my sandwich. I make three like this: for Otis, for you, for me.

Faces and bodies become estranged in the flickering fire light, and goose-bumping proximity is more intimate than eye contact, than talking. Cheap wine, a bottle of vodka, a joint are passed around. By the time it comes to me, the roach is supple and moist. When the legs come round me, one on either side like an armrest, at first I do not know it's you. It's only when you whisper "Feeling anything yet?" that I settle into the shape you form for me. I tell you earnestly about the fairy houses in the logs, the glowing white windows that show someone is home. I say there are little doors in tree roots that have lifted from the ground. I have seen some today. I reach my hands up to find your face, glance your furred belly, warm beneath your t-shirt. You slip off the log, so your belly is pressed against my back. Your arms come down around me, thumbs brushing my forearms. I am small between your legs, my legs stretched out inside the diamond of your limbs. Your hand slips down inside my dungarees, and rests there, tracing the seam where my torso meets my hip. I lean my cheek upon your knee. The denim is cool and damp. The fire has petals. It is made of silk, I think. Occasionally it illuminates a single face, floating in the air like a mask. One with full flower lips that bobs and hits against another mask, with a thick brow. Candlemas eyes, clustered in the dark, like fireflies. Green, yellow. A small body - must be Daisy - dances like a pixie, sashaying her hips, this way, that way, this, in front of him then falls into the lap of shadow and I only see her feet from then, her bare toes wiggling, her socks left drying by the fireside. I mumble that I want to go back to the tent. I don't think you hear me, so I whisper it again. I say: "Soon I'll be back in London and you'll be back at school with them. They can have you then. But for now, can we just -"

A voice in the distant dark suggests a game. There are groans and whoops of approval. We're too old for spin the bottle. Not that, not that. A good game. I can't pick out where one voice ends and another begins. Only a strange cacophony of gurgled murmurs, sudden yawps, and an airy echo which seems to come from me. We all stand up, and stagger round. Some kind of hide and seek, I guess. I stumble down the track. Everything is purple-black, except the wood anemones which shine bright white all along the path. Fairies. The split of twigs. I walk faster, grabbing hold of the trees and swinging my weight from trunk to trunk. The trees step back and push me forward into a clearing. There, I stop. The white rutting of an arse and her blonde hair like the sun's silk threads caught on the bracken and unravelled, pulled into a frizz.

"Daisy?" I blink hard twice, a toady blink, and step backwards into the dark. The sky glimpsed between the trees still holds some light. It is deep blue but veined with brooding, blacker clouds. The fire, far away now, is an astigmatic star; light stretching in four directions around the globe of my eye. North. I am sealegged. Sailors squinting into the endless black, horizonless black, thinking moonbeams on the waves are constellations from their maps. I have been treading water. Where are you? You must be somewhere. I am someway into the woods now and the outlines of each tree has changed.

They have rearranged themselves like grandma's footsteps. I rest my hand on one. Its craggy surface is familiar so I stroke it, hoping it tells me where to go. I let my head loll forwards. Bile swims up. I can't open my eyes. My mouth opens and closes, gagging like a codfish, coward, coquettish little sick.

A body behind me now. I let myself roll against it. Warm. Broad. Tall with hands that reach around me. You found me. Have you been hiding?
"That was the game," I say and find I am too gone to know if that is what I mean. Where have *you* been?

But this hand scrunched around my breast, hoiking it out of my bra, is larger than yours, blunt thumbed and rough skinned. I catch the glinting of a ring but I think it's the wrong hand. This hand is left, twisting and tugging at my nipple as I wince. This hand is full of clay and earth and rabbit shit. The breath too like mildew. And the scent, like acetone and sweat. Deodorant and pond. The other hand grips tighter to my hip, slides down around my arse and hooks inside me. My body is a choking fish. My mouth opens. My yelp clags under my tongue like the sand of chewing sloes. Silent as a leech, it presses into me. A clownish root unbalances me. My ankle, I protest. It's hard to know if I am talking out loud. I am dropped to the ground, onto the bluebell bed, into the thick, damp scent of healthful rot and leaf mould between my lips. I see them now. The feet strapped in dark shoes, an orange tick, with jeans pooled round, crushing bluebells unthinkingly. Each bluebell takes seven years to grow from seed to bloom. Did you know that? And now their necks are cracked. They emit their heady glue. My mouth is full with it. I pull back, away, sniffling into the dark like a mouse. A shadow looms towards me, saying shhh like wind through the leaves, huh the saw through the wood. Shh, huh, shh. Blood pulsing in my head, in my belly, in my chest. The unfamiliar thickness of the neck as I reach up and slip my hand around this throat, which splutters with the shock, spraying me with spit. The eyes spring open, white in the dark. And then a flick of blue. These eyes I know. I know *you*.

I scrabbled away to the edge of the forest and there I lay on my back and looked at the sky until I needed to be sick. I turned onto my side, foetal, and vomited into the bluebell mess.

I woke there, hours later and corpse cold. My legs were fishnetted with lacerations from the brambles. My face was streaked with wet ash. I remember the birds chattering violently. The rich brimstone stink and grey smocked sky of the surrounding moor, alight. I lifted myself onto my unsteady feet and wandered out into the field. No one else was awake, it seemed, except a cuckoo, who sang as she threw eggs onto the ground. The gorse crackled and snarked as the horizon turned a luminous, devilish red, like a sun rising in the West. My hand ached so much, I thought it might be broken. The following day I'll learn that it's just strained. In the newspaper, I will hear that you passed out drunk, and I looked everywhere for you before the smoke got too thick to see. The trees were coming down all around me. They made a sound like breaking bones. Everyone will say, and it will be true: there was nothing else that I could do.

I stand in the field. The ash falls like snow, settling on my skin, and I watch, as the sky catches.

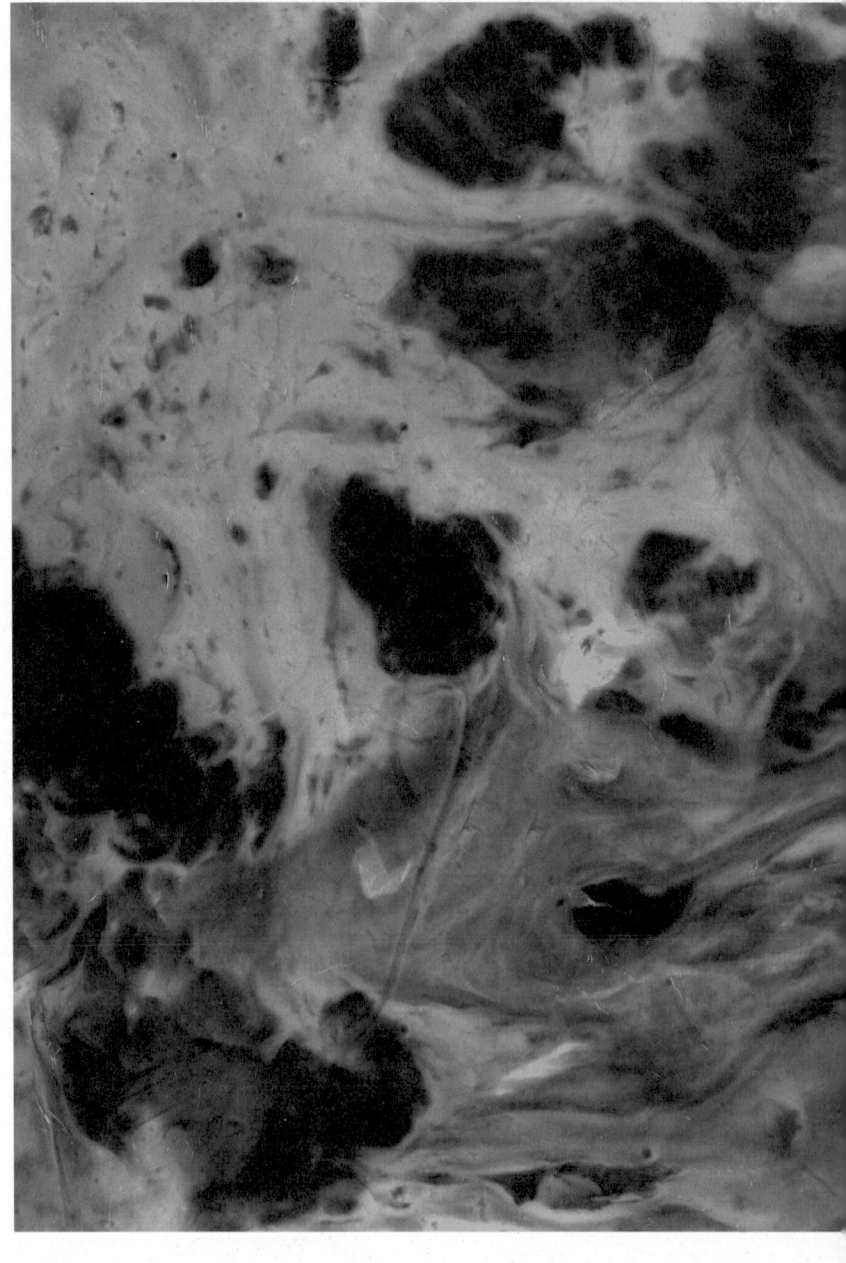

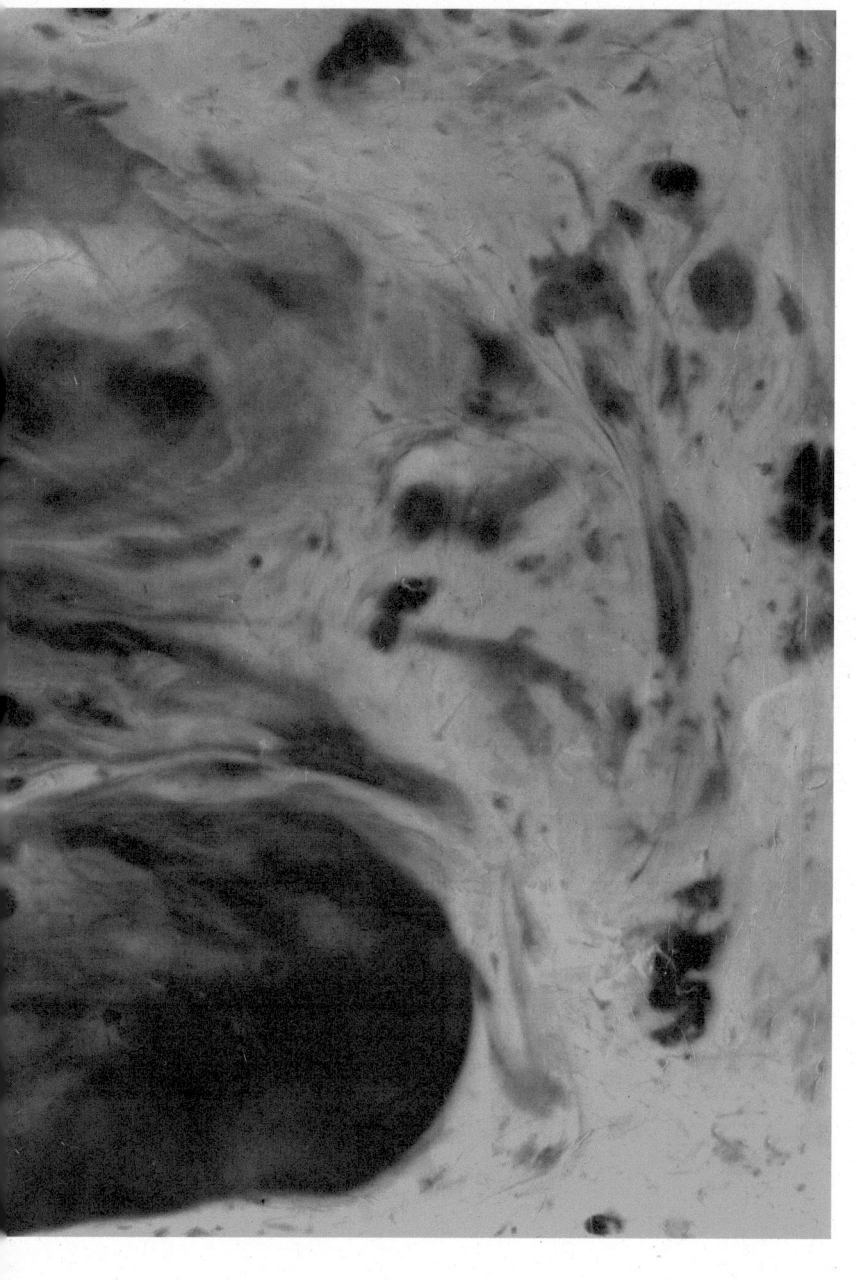

12:50

It is January and it has been snowing. You step out into the garden to eye the frost that glitters on the rotting leaves. You hope the cat will go out to wee. Instead, she sits at your feet, drumming her tail against your leg. She places a paw gingerly on the icy threshold and then withdraws it. You draw the door closed again. You breathe into your palms. Today is Monday, the day of your appointment.

This appointment has been in your diary for a week. Seven days since that brown envelope came through the old brush-mouthed letterbox that sounds like it's saying 'fed-up'. You copied the time and address into your diary. You check it now. The blue biro remains unmoved. 12:50. Your daughter told you there would be a lot of waiting.

You leave the house at midday to walk to the hospital. The half hour walk takes twice that long because of the ice. The ice has grown cowboyish, roughly assembled from layers of slush wetted down with grit and frozen again. The black cat slips between your legs as you close the door. She pads ahead, then pounces so her front legs descend into the thickest mound of gutter snow. You did not know she was capable of such kittenish frivolity. You bend to scratch her under the chin. She shivers her whiskers and springs onto a low wall to preen. You nod to her as you waddle on, hands held out for balance.

You creep down the hill, gloved fingers groping for purchase on brick walls. "The half hour walk took twice that long," you explain to the receptionist when you arrive. She says, "Don't worry, there might be a bit of a wait anyway."

16:40

Hours later, when you emerge, the sun has given way to dusk. You stand outside the hospital, eyes casting about in the white. The road is flanked by sheep fleeced trees. You step out. A bike skids past you, narrowly. You totter on, muttering a rosary of oh dears. The flat lawn of the methodist church is shrouded in snow except for a diagonal path, trodden and dog-tracked. You turn your head up into the sky to feel the snowflakes melt upon your nose. They catch softly on your eyelashes. The tears are breaching. Your feet give. Your toes lift from the ground, weight thrown back onto your ankles. Your hips strain in their sockets, croaking, and then with a sudden spearlike pain, your coccyx hits the hardened ground. You do not bounce. You split. Bone gape, pink, the jam of it. You squall, fox screech. On all fours, you shuffle into the doorway of the church, and tuck your nose into your armpit. More bikes skim past. You phone your daughter. She picks up. You barely speak before she says, "Stay there, I'm coming."

12:15

Thick, blue haematomas encircle her breast. She has unclasped her bra, wiggled it down her arms. She turns from me to rummage through her underwear drawer for something more comfortable for lunch. On her back, I note the pink imprints of the straps in her white flesh. The chain of moles that twinkle down her spine. The smear of red at the small of her back where the scab is flaking. The black cotton and strained elastic of her knickers. Her right foot rising up her left calf to scratch some legion of irritation. The mole on the side of her big toe. The cracks in her yellowed heels. The blue mycelial veins beneath her skin, bluer in the tender hinge of the knee, the elbow, the armpit. When she raises her arms above her head to pin her hair up, the lacing of those fine blonde hairs at her stem.

12:27

The deputy's soft fist is poised to knock. He slips his mouth close to the crack and asks, "May I come in?" "Almost," comes the reply. His fingers flex on the handle. "Come in," now she is undressed, the woman on the bed. She is sat up, with her arms crossed over herself. She has shimmied her shoulders out of her jumper so it slumps around the softness of her belly. Her t-shirt, navy, has been struggled off and dropped to the floor in a heap. Above it, her swinging feet. Her bra folded so its cups nest within each other, placed carefully behind her on the bed. He sits down on the stool opposite her. It squeaks on its wheels. He clicks the mouse rapidly until the screen buzzes into light and skims her notes to find the scan. The titanium marker glowing white amongst the shadowy legions. He uncaps the pen and approaches her, eyes still trained on the computer screen. Her breast, her left. The last bruises, like watermarks, are fading around the areole. Her breast is flattened against her sternum and heavier at the bottom. She looks over his head to a poster on the wall about counselling. A faded picture of clasped hands which could have been plucked from a funeral directors' brochure. He measures

213

10mm below and 90mm across. Holds the skin taut with his fingers in an L. One line down. Lift. One line across. There. The ink pools slightly in her wrinkles and stretch marks. She looks down at the cross for a moment. He slips the pen back into his pocket and begins typing up his notes. "Is that all?" she asks, and, though he knows there is much more to come, he turns and nods and smiles, and then he stands and leaves her to get dressed.

12:32

If motherhood had a smell it would be mashed banana and cat piss. It embeds itself into your nostrils during that post-partum fug. I haven't been able to shake it since. I wake up from my nap, wrinkle my nose, and text my daughter. I wait for her reply. I walk around the house, sniffing. I search all the private and carpeted corners that the cat might have pissed. I shine a torch into the closet, under the bed. I get on my hands and knees to look under the bath. I pat my handbag, suspect dampness, and bring it to my nose. I fill the cat's bowl with biscuits and narrow my eyes at her as I place it down. She weaves about my ankles, tail tickling my knees. I sniff my armpit, worried for a moment that the ammonia stench is coming from me.

I open the door and fan it to get the air flowing through the kitchen. I step into the garden and check the flagstones for thawing fox shit. It could be a dead mouse in the drains. The cat has taken to drowning them that way. I am both proud and wary of her progression to tools. I lift the grate off the drain, taking my phone out of my pocket for the torch.

My daughter has texted back. She would still love to go for lunch. I abandon the drain, leaving the grate in a puddle on the side. I text as I walk: we'll go to the nice place (which doesn't smell of cat piss.) I'll drive. It isn't a long walk, but it's cold and we both get tired. My daughter wouldn't even eat bananas when she was a baby. The cat chirrups as she follows me up the stairs. She rubs her cheek on the carpet outside the bathroom, measuring it up.

17:20

It has been three days since she came back from the hospital. She still complains of the latex scent from the anaesthesiologist's gloves that she can't get out of her nose. She also complains about the grease in her hair, and runs her palm over it, grimacing. She mutters that both would be solved by a bath. The wound still wet enough itself that it must be kept dry. Mostly she is asleep when I visit. She sleeps all afternoon. When she sleeps, the cat does not knead her chest but lies beside her, nuzzling her palm. Her palm as pale as a magnolia petal, curling, timorous, by the cat's hot nose. I sit with her feet in my lap. I pop two codeine pills out of their silver foil and give them to her. She swallows them with a gasp. She falls asleep again, her mouth still suckling the air. I fiddle all her hospital letters and prescription scripts into a plastic sleeve. All week, she sleeps like a baby, and shits hard pellets like a rabbit.

12:48

Service is slow. It's the snow. It was hard enough for me to get in. Getting home will be worse. No buses. Meant to snow

215

again. I've had eyes on the clock, elbow on the counter, stiff back from the draught all day. It's 12:50. I could have done with an extra hour this morning.

The door swings open. I say "sit anywhere," gesturing to the table by the window. They sit, in hushed silence. The daughter has bags under her eyes, and the back of her hair is fuzzy with sleep. The mother keeps rising off the seat, then sitting back down, then rising again. She whispers to her daughter, "Do we order at the counter?" I pick up two menus. They are watery eyed with gratitude. One americano. One cappuccino, no chocolate. They both order marmite toast with poached eggs. I rip the page from the pad, and poke my head into the kitchen to grin at Paul. He is hanging out the back door, having a fag. I click my fingers and hold the page aloft. Smiling, he snatches it from my hands and digs me in the ribs. I swish my ponytail as I leave.

The daughter is nodding. I hear her telling her mother that, "It will be over soon." They are grateful that the cafe is quiet. If I were going to have a conversation about cancer in a cafe, I'd come on Saturday, between ten and one, when amongst the din no one would pick out a single word I said. They thank me for the eggs when I collect their plates. The mother signals for the bill. I tot it up.

13:00

When I was little, you took my head in your palm and lowered me into the water. You lathered shampoo in your palms and spidered your hands, scrunching the bubbles through my hair. You held your wrist over my brow, tipped my chin back

216

and poured jugfuls of water over my head, until the water ran clear. My eyes squeezed shut, toes curling, mouth open slightly, and in one hand, a barbie face down, her swimming costume soaked right through. I remember the pleasure of a flannel being rung out over my back. The softness of your grip, lifting my arms to soap my armpits. The almost suffocation of the flannel swiped over my face, and round my ears, and how cold the air was on my damp cheeks when it was done. I remember the bath towel wrapped around me, and as you turned away, my palm reaching for your face to call you back to me, your eyes to mine, demanding that you keep on being my "Mummy" now, and now, and now, and now, again.

We are in the bathroom. You sit on a chair by the sink. I run the taps and scoop water over your head. I wash your hair gently, careful not to get soap in your eyes. When I have combed the conditioner through, you sit up for a while with the licked ribbon of your hair coiled stickily over your collar bone. We nurse cups of tea, and talk about platelets, new flats, bio oil, sports bras, work, the bulbs you've planted, and the squirrel who keeps digging them up. When you are ready, I rinse. Wrist shielding your brow and warm cupfuls of water, over and over until the water runs clear down the plug hole.

14:45

The patients that come to physiotherapy are tired. In this corner of the hospital, the word tired is a cipher that means pain and disappointment as much as it means sleepless. Years into detailing their symptoms, they all end up with tired. It means burdened. It means in need of rest. I ask them to close their eyes, eyelids fluttering with focus, to stand on one leg and to touch their nose with their index finger. I kneel down and ask them to try and hold their ankles still. We bend their legs, one by one. We flex their wrists. Make fists. Unclench and start again. I look at her posture when she comes in and I ask if she would like a glass of water. She apologises for being late. She explains that she was having lunch with her mother. She seems embarrassed to admit that they go for lunch most weeks. I tell her that I have dinner with my sister every Tuesday. She says, "That's nice." I take her foot in my hand and tell her to push against me as hard as she can. She apologises for not having practised. She says she has been struggling to get out of bed in the morning. The cold doesn't help. The ice makes her anxious. She slipped on the road on her way in today and her hip is still throbbing. Instead, she just lies in bed for hours, the pain beating its way along her bones. She waits for the reprieve to come, until time gets banjaxed and her body starts aching freshly from its flatness. I show her some gentle stretches that she can do in bed. Her back twisted away from me, she says: "My mother has just been diagnosed with breast cancer." She turns her head back to me. "I feel bad saying this, but I am jealous. She's had four appointments already. There's just so much they can do." I ask her to relax her hands. Then I say: "We're doing something now, for you."

12:50

My mother takes me to the nice place again. We both order marmite toast and poached eggs. We walked here through the park, crunching twigs beneath our feet. I wandered ahead a while, until I lost the sense of her. Then I slowed. Catching up, she slipped her arm through mine, and smiled her cat smile as she asked if I was "making up a story." I remember how I used to dander ahead when I was small. Some of these memories were told to me, later on. I had been thinking about this winter and how slowly it was easing into spring. We walk on, side by side. We talk about the horrible colour they paint hospital walls. It is ten to one. I could be five. The velvety pendulum swing of her voice. The first green leaves of the crocuses lilting in the breeze.

Acknowledgements

This book was commissioned by Ned Green at Toothgrinder Press in 2022. He has treated it with gentleness and braying enthusiasm since the beginning. Huge thanks to William Green for designing and illustrating this beautiful book, and to my dear Jack Davison for letting us use his photographs.

I cannot thank John Livesy enough for spurring me to write *AMPHIBIAN* in 2021. I had twelve days to write the script, after a slot at the Playmill Festival opened up. John stayed on speakerphone while I edited, making encouraging sounds. I should thank John too for cracking an egg onto an overhead projector. The egg scans were recreated for this book by William Green, based on John's original concept. Thanks also to Natalie Quarry, Louis Grace, Issey Gladston, Max Cadman, Stephen Hagan, and everyone who brought *AMPHIBIAN* to life on stage - twice.

Thank you to Laura Stimson, Megan Bradbury, the UEA New Forms Award judges who awarded me the prize, and everyone at the National Centre for Writing.

Endless gratitude to Roz, Evie and Ben at Review in Peckham for letting me write behind the till.

And big grins reserved for everyone at Blue Shout Poetry, Gob Jaw, Yer Bard and all the other great open mic nights, where I read foetal versions of these stories. Thank you Angus for geeing up the crowd.

This is a book about bodies, so I must thank my exceptional lockdown GP, Dr English, whom I have never met, who researched my conditions and prescribed me life changing meds, as well as all the physios, nurses, pharmacists, receptionists, and junior doctors who have restored my faith in medicine and helped lessen the pain.

Thank you also to BPAS, and every organisation that provides abortion care with kindness and without judgment. Thank you to the people who have shared their abortion stories with me.

I am very grateful for my friendship with my Mum, Serena, and my Dad, Simon. My brothers - Sasha, Saul, & Joe. My aunt Flora, Johnny, Marina and Ralph at the Neptune's Cave. Grace, Iris and Bea. My inimitable grandparents; Brian for always asking what I am writing; Granny Fiona for making me literally piss with laughter; Miranda - Granny Yorkshire - for the doll's house where I staged my first domestic dramas. And the dogs - the late Frida and the young Zonky - both big fans of the woods.

All my friends, but especially: Kitty L, who offered me advice on naming sea monsters in Latin and Greek. Joy, who brought African clawed frogs to my attention. Kitty D, Helena, Esther, Matty, Talia, Maisy, Gazelle, Billie, Zara, Maya; I would rot in my bedroom without you. And my Daniel; thank you for buying me flowers on the way to the clinic.

Thank you to everyone who must trust, against the evidence, that I haven't written about them.

You are all good toads.

Vida Adamczewski was born in Peckham, South East London. She read Politics, Philosophy and Economics at the University of Oxford, graduating in 2019. Vida's writing has appeared in *Ambit Magazine*, *Document Journal*, *Vittles* and *The Mays*. In July 2021, a staged reading of Vida's debut lyric play *AMPHIBIAN* was performed at the Playmill New Writers Festival at the King's Head Theatre in Islington. For *AMPHIBIAN*, Vida was awarded the UEA New Forms Award 2022 by the National Centre for Writing. *Amphibian and Other Bodies* is her first collection.